"I driv

Cara said, her eyes lighting up with impish interest. "How amazing."

"You don't have to sound so thrilled about it," Rod muttered.

"Hey, I would have settled for respect, but since you seem reluctant to bestow that, I'll take driving you crazy. At least that means you're hearing me."

"Oh, I'm hearing you loud and clear, and I don't like it one bit." His voice began to rise. With great restraint he lowered it to what he hoped would be a threatening growl. "Now maybe you'd like to listen to me. You will be on that plane out of here this afternoon if I have to tie you to the seat."

"You and whose army?" she inquired, curious.

"Dammit, woman!"

"You swear entirely too much."

He rubbed his head, which was beginning to pound like the very devil. "Especially since you arrived, princess," he conceded.

Dear Reader,

Magic. It dazzles our senses, sometimes touches our souls. And what could be more magical than romance?

Silhouette **Special Edition** novels feature believable, compelling women and men in lifelike situations, but our authors never forget the wondrous magic of falling in love. How do these writers blend believability with enchantment? Author Sherryl Woods puts it this way:

"More. That's what Silhouette **Special Edition** is about. For a writer, this Silhouette line offers a chance to create romances with more depth and complexity, more intriguing characters, more heightened sensuality. In the pages of these wonderful love stories, more sensitive issues can be interwoven with more tenderness, more humor and more excitement. And when it all works, you have what these books are really all about—more magic!"

Joining Sherryl Woods this month to conjure up half a dozen versions of this "special" magic are Robyn Carr, Debbie Macomber, Barbara Catlin, Maggi Charles and Jennifer Mikels.

Month after month, we hope Silhouette **Special Edition** casts its spell on you, dazzling your senses *and* touching your soul. Are there any particular ingredients you like best in your "love potion"? The authors and editors of Silhouette **Special Edition** always welcome your comments.

Sincerely,

Leslie Kazanjian, Senior Editor
Silhouette Books
300 East 42nd Street
New York, N.Y. 10017

SHERRYL WOODS
In
Too Deep

Silhouette Special Edition

Published by Silhouette Books New York

America's Publisher of Contemporary Romance

To Dan...
for all the adventures

SILHOUETTE BOOKS
300 East 42nd St., New York, N.Y. 10017

ISBN: 0-373-09522-8

First Silhouette Books printing April 1989

Printed in the U.S.A.

Books by Sherryl Woods

Silhouette Desire

Not at Eight, Darling #309
Yesterday's Love #329
Come Fly with Me #345
A Gift of Love #375
Can't Say No #431
Heartland #472

Silhouette Special Edition

Safe Harbor #425
Never Let Go #446
Edge of Forever #484
In Too Deep #522

SHERRYL WOODS

lives by the ocean, which, she says, provides daily inspiration for the romance in her soul. She further explains that her years as a television critic taught her about steamy plots and humor; her years as a travel editor took her to exotic locations; and her years as a crummy weekend tennis player taught her to stick with what she enjoyed most—writing. "What better way is there," Sherryl asks, "to combine all that experience than by creating romantic stories?"

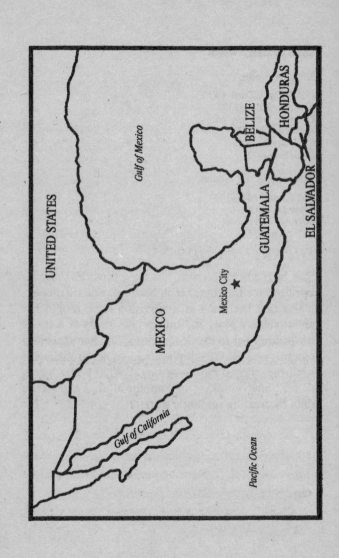

Prologue

William Harrington Scott, what do you think you're doing?"

Cara's outraged voice carried all the way down the hospital corridor. Her father frantically tried to shove what appeared to be an entire file drawer's contents out of sight under the sheets. Spots of guilty color rose on his pale cheeks.

"Are you trying to kill yourself?" she demanded, crossing the room in three furious strides and yanking at the sheet. Scottie held on tight. His strength was clearly returning. She was no match for it.

"Stop acting like a mother hen," he grumbled. "It's just a few files."

"Hand 'em over." Retreating from the physical stalemate, she attempted psychological warfare. She simply held out her hand and waited.

Her wily father was up to that game, too. He folded his arms across his chest in a familiar gesture meant to convey that he was quite capable of outwaiting her. Cara returned his scowl with a pleasant smile. His gaze narrowed.

"Don't think you can outfox me, missy. I was getting my way long before you were even born. Now stop all this nonsense and explain to me why there isn't a report in here from Rod Craig. The Mexicans wanted that dam survey completed by June first."

"I'm aware of the deadline," she retorted defensively, then could have kicked herself for confirming what Scottie had already guessed: the report was overdue by nearly two weeks. Since there seemed no way around the discussion, she added, "There hasn't been a word from Craig in the last month. I've told you before you've given the man entirely too much freedom."

"He does his job," Scottie countered, then amended, "usually."

His expression grew thoughtful. Thinking he was distracted, Cara made a grab for the thick Usumacinta dam project file from which the Craig report was conspicuously absent. Scottie easily deflected her hands. She put them on her hips and glowered at him.

"Then why wasn't that survey on your desk at least three weeks ago?" she demanded. "If it had been, it would have been ready to be passed on to the Mexican government on schedule. Craig knew the deadline. It came and went without so much as a phone call from your *reliable* protégé. If it had been anyone else, you'd have been bellowing so loud you'd be heard clear across the border.''

"I don't like it," Scottie admitted, letting down his guard. Cara grabbed again and this time she got the folder away from the bed. She clutched it tightly, while her father continued to grumble. "Craig may be a pain in the butt, but he's never been late on a project before. He sure as hell has kept me informed. Are you sure he hasn't called? Maybe someone forgot to give you the message."

Cara regarded him skeptically. "Louise? You know better. Your secretary is so efficient she could make the airlines run on time."

The comment didn't draw so much as a grin. "I don't like it one bit, Cara. There's something weird going on down there or we'd have heard from him by now."

He still wasn't bellowing. In fact, Cara was surprised by the note of genuine concern in her father's voice. As she regarded him curiously, he scowled at her and made a lunge for the Usumacinta papers. His movements were hindered by the IV attached to his arm. She stepped deftly aside, put the file safely out of reach, then returned to gather up the rest of the reports.

"Give me back those papers," Scottie growled, but it was a halfhearted protest.

"You're not supposed to be working, Scottie. If I find out who brought these to you, I'm going to fire them." She knew perfectly well who the guilty party was—Louise. The woman would scale mountains if Scottie asked her to.

"Dammit, girl, WHS Engineering is still my company."

"Assuming you live long enough to run it. Dr. Atkins says you shouldn't be upset."

"Louise wouldn't have brought those reports if..." His voice floundered guiltily.

Cara grinned triumphantly. "So that is who it was. I'm not surprised. When are you going to stop asking that lovely lady to do all your dirty work?"

"Hell's bells, girl, that's what I pay her for."

"I don't think she does it for the money," she retorted, drawing a puzzled look from her father. The man was definitely obtuse. Louise absolutely worshiped the ground he trod on with his muddy boots. Cara, on the other hand, was not such an easy mark. She braced herself for more badgering.

"I'm telling you the doctor said it would be okay for me to read a little. He told Louise."

"Fine. I'll bring you a mystery."

He tried a pathetic look on for size. Cara ignored it. He wheedled. "Come on, Cara. Do this for your old man. You know I hate fiction."

"I am doing it for my old man. Maybe it's time you learned to appreciate Agatha Christie. Maybe, when you're stronger, some Sidney Sheldon or Jackie Collins. Meantime, I am taking these reports and leaving here so you'll get some rest.''

He sagged in defeat. She leaned down then and kissed him, determined to leave before he could see how frightened she was by his unnatural gray pallor, the quick waning of his energy. Before the heart attack, Scottie would have chased her around the room for those files. Now he seemed willing to give up after a relatively mild verbal skirmish.

She tried to remember how much better he was already, but it didn't help. Her heart seemed to lodge in her throat every time she walked through the door to his room. Ever since the nearly fatal heart attack had felled her boisterous, vital father four weeks earlier, she'd felt like a child again, terrified by the prospect of being left alone. It had been worse when he'd been in intensive care, lying so incredibly still, the tentative rhythm of his life monitored by machine. She'd tried desperately then to keep her gaze averted from the equipment, but simply holding Scottie's huge, callused hand in hers had brought tears to her eyes. The faint squeezes he'd given in response to her reassurances had been pale, unsatisfactory imitations of his hearty hugs.

He really was better now, but the visits still left her shaken. She knew, though, that Scottie would be bewildered by her reaction. Despite its severity, he didn't see the attack as an ominous sign of his mortality. In fact, he was taking the whole thing in stride, already chomping at the bit to get on with his life. As far as he was concerned this had been no more than a damned inconvenience.

"Sleep," she ordered.

"Who the hell can sleep when people keep hiding things? Get on the phone and find out what's going on down in Mexico."

"I'll find out, Scottie," she promised. Then she winked. "But I won't tell you unless you behave."

She spent the next forty-eight hours in a frustrating attempt to get the answers she and her father wanted. Efforts to reach Rod Craig by radiophone proved futile. According to the hotel where he'd based himself in Palenque, he'd been in the field for the past three weeks. They hadn't heard from him, either.

She hung up after her last call and stared out the window. Scottie wasn't going to rest until he knew what was going on. For that matter, neither was she, and it was up to her to find out. She searched her desktop for the scheduling sheet for the engineers on staff. Not a one of them was available for an emergency trip to Mexico.

If she wanted immediate answers, that left one alternative. She buzzed for Louise.

"I'm going to Mexico," she announced, while flipping through the flight schedules she kept on file. "Make the arrangements and get whatever supplies I'll need. I'll go home for my passport, pack a bag and be back here in an hour. I want to leave on the afternoon flight."

Used to Scottie's spur-of-the-moment decisions, the attractive brunet secretary never even blinked at Cara's impromptu plans. She began jotting down Cara's instructions and added a few of her own.

"That does it, then," Louise said, when *she* was satisfied. Cara grinned at the secretary's smooth takeover of the planning.

"I'll have your ticket when you get back," Louise promised. She started for the door, then turned back. An expression of concern filled her sparkling brown eyes. "Does your father know?"

"I'll call him from the airport."

When she made that call several hours later, Scottie was not nearly as enthusiastic about the decision as she'd anticipated he would be. Silence greeted the announcement.

"What's wrong?"

"Maybe you should send Mark," he suggested finally.

"I thought about that but Mark's in Brazil. He's right at a critical stage of the work down there. He couldn't fly up till the end of the month. We can't wait that long."

"Hank, then."

"You know perfectly well that Hank's in Cairo. Everyone else is tied up, too. I'm going, Scottie. I can be there in twenty-four hours. I can assess things just as well as they can." That, of course, was the crux of the matter. She still had this ridiculous need to prove herself to her father, to win his approval along with his love.

He muttered an exasperated curse, and she knew he had seen right through her.

"Dammit, girl, I know you're a good engineer or I wouldn't have made you a vice president, but you ain't used to tromping around in the jungle."

"I'll manage," she said with what she hoped was enough confidence to reassure him. "I made that trip to Brazil with you, didn't I? I didn't even faint when I found that snake in my bedroll."

"No. You just screamed your fool head off till I came running. What'll you do this time? I'm not going to be there."

"Scottie, I'm only going for a day or so. As long as I don't fall into a snake pit, I'll be just fine."

"And what if you do?"

"Do what?"

"Fall into a snake pit?"

"Scottie, I was joking."

"I'm not. You don't know what the hell you're likely to run into down there. There could be wild savages in that jungle."

"We're talking about Mexico, not the interior of Africa."

"Okay, then, bandits."

"You're the one who taught me how to defend myself. I've packed my malaria pills. I have a snake-bite kit. I'll buy bottled water and cans of food in Palenque."

"Hiking boots?"

"I have them."

"What about a hat?"

"It's in my hand."

"Mosquito netting?"

"Scottie, I sent Louise shopping."

"Then you have everything." He sighed, though she wasn't certain whether it was in resignation or satisfaction.

"What about Craig, though? How're you gonna handle him? He's not like those guys you're used to ordering around at the office or leading around on a dance floor. He won't quake in his boots the minute you lift one of those eyebrows the way you do when you're about to lose your cool."

"How difficult can he be? He works for us, not the other way around."

"He works for us precisely because I leave him alone to do the job I pay him for. Rod Craig's his own man, missy, and you'd be doing well not to forget it."

It was only after she was in the air that she wondered what the hell her father had meant by that.

Chapter One

Dear God in heaven, there really was a jungle down there, Cara thought, staring out the filthy airplane window with a sort of horrified fascination. Brilliant shades of emerald green splashed across shadowed hues of olive. This wasn't the idyllic green of an un-expected patch of sunlit grass discovered deep in the forest. Nor was it the rich, darkly mysterious color of rain-soaked valleys in Ireland. This was an endless, undulating sea of tangled vines and elephantine leaves, of impenetrable undergrowth and hidden dangers.

"What did you expect?" she muttered under her breath. "Central Park?"

Actually, that would have been nice. In fact, it would have been terrific to be in Central Park right now, jogging along a familiar paved path. She loved being surrounded by the towering skyscrapers of civilization, listening to a Mozart tape as she ran. At this hour she'd be close to home again, just starting to anticipate the day's first savory cup of her favorite special blend of coffee, a buttery croissant with thick raspberry jam and the *Wall Street Journal*.

Instead, she was heading deep into the Mexican rain forest in search of a man everyone had been telling her for years now was an independent, arrogant, bullheaded rogue. The company gossip about the man's professional and amatory exploits was the stuff of which legends were made. Even her father had said that Rod Craig was nothing but trouble. What confused her slightly was that her father's voice held a note of envy when he said it.

From the moment she'd heard it while still in her teens, that unexpected note had intrigued her. Scottie, who'd founded WHS Engineering nearly thirty years ago, had a well-documented independent streak of his own. He envied few men. That alone, then, would have been enough to make her curious, but that wasn't all. In some way she couldn't quite define—and didn't like admitting—her father's apparent affection and admiration for Rod Craig also hurt her. It reminded her that there was a time in his life she hadn't shared, a carefree time that Rod epitomized and her father still, after all these years, longed for. This life they had in New York was second best to her father.

Now Cara was about to find out for herself if Rod Craig lived up to his reputation. After a four-hour delay on the ground in New York, two flights, a hair-raising drive over twisting mountain roads and a night in a bug-infested room in Palenque, she was back in the air in some plane that looked like it had been patched together with Krazy Glue and rubber bands. The hotel manager had reluctantly arranged the charter. Amid muttered prayers to all the saints, he had also drawn her a map of the area along the river where she was likely to find Rod.

She'd studied the sketch carefully, asked several questions, then nodded in satisfaction. It appeared straightforward enough, a walk of perhaps a mile, maybe two from the airstrip. It was hardly the dangerous or physically taxing venture her father had feared. She walked farther than that between appointments in New York. She'd hiked more treacherous distances on sites in the desert. She was accustomed to getting along on unfamiliar terrain. Scottie had taught her well. The hotel manager had remained horrified by her blasé attitude. She wrote it off, first to Latin machismo, then to avarice.

"Please, señorita, you go by boat. I find you best guide," he had argued. "Normally he take tours on the river, but for you special deal."

Scottie's concern echoed through her mind. "How long to arrange it?"

"Two, maybe three days, he be back."

"I'll go by plane."

"It is dangerous, señorita, no place for a woman alone."

"Give me the map."

More prayers had been muttered for her stubborn soul. As the plane dipped and swayed, she was beginning to be thankful for the manager's communications on her behalf. It was going to take a heavenly influence to keep her alive on this flight. And she very much wanted to live, just so she could kill Rod Craig for causing all this inconvenience.

Carlos, the pilot, had the look of a bandit with a streak of the daredevil in his soul. He'd been lavishing gap-toothed smiles on her since takeoff. With the plane's engine coughing and sputtering, they were flying awfully low over this endless, intimidating jungle, which should have required enough attention to keep his mind off her. Instead, he seemed determined to terrify her with his aerial acrobatics.

She sat back and closed her eyes. Despite her appearance of calm, this was not the sort of adventure she relished. She'd never admitted it to Scottie, but she preferred the challenge of the boardroom or the excitement of her drawing board. Those were the things she understood, things she could control. Though she'd done fieldwork with Scottie and was more than qualified for this assignment, it was not the aspect of her job she preferred.

As a result of her present anxiety and the unappealing prospect of worse to come, Cara was in no mood to deal politely with some irresponsible rake who was off in the wilderness indulging his lusty li-

bido on company time. If it had been up to her, she'd
have fired the man, but that would have upset her father, and she would not have Scottie worrying himself into another heart attack. So, instead, she was
going to get this project moving if she had to join
ranks with Rod or, if he didn't like that, simply do it
herself.

Suddenly the plane dove downward into a tiny
clearing. Her heart thumping wildly, Cara watched
wide-eyed as Carlos landed on a cleared stretch of dirt
that had been barely visible from the air and was not
one inch longer than it needed to be. The trees and
vines seemed to close in around them. Though the sun
was high in the midday sky, it was filtered by the
density of the greenery, reaching the ground in pale
fingers. She swallowed hard and wondered exactly
what the hell she'd gotten herself into.

"Which way, Carlos?"

He pointed her toward a narrow dirt path barely
visible in the wild undergrowth and towering mahogany trees. If it had ever been intended as a road, time
had choked off its potential.

"No problem," he said, grinning broadly. Cara
spoke perfectly fluent Spanish, but Carlos had insisted on practicing his English. "One hour. Maybe
less. You find river. Señor Craig, he be there. Somewhere. Maybe."

Her heart thumped irregularly at the vague quali-
fication.

Sensing her hesitation, he added, "One hundred
dollars American, I take you."

It was a tempting offer, but the price seemed outrageously high just for the comfort of having someone to walk with for an hour or so.

"You just be back here tomorrow afternoon," she told him.

Carlos's bright brown eyes regarded her with respect. "You very brave señorita. You have a man at home?"

"No man," she confessed.

"This Señor Craig, he your man?"

"Hardly."

He nodded sympathetically. "Take very strong man to be good for you, lady. My brother, he very strong. You want to meet?"

Cara laughed at his hopeful expression. "No, thank you, Carlos. I'm not looking for a man in my life right now."

He shook his head. "Not good to be without a man. Man-woman is way it is meant to be. You think about what I say. We talk again tomorrow."

Then he was gone. She was surprised to feel a lump in her throat as she watched him fly away. She stood gazing after the plane until it was no more than a spark of light glinting through that narrow slit to the distant sky.

When she could avoid it no longer, she took a slow look around and shuddered. The landing strip was no more than a deserted stretch of cleared ground. The small tin-sided shack fifty yards away had an abandoned air about it. The only sounds were the wild shrieks of birds she couldn't even see in the dense foliage. Storm clouds were gathering, temporarily muting the full force of the hot sun. She suddenly felt incredibly lonely and far, far out of her element.

"I really don't like this," she muttered, but she determinedly picked up her small flight bag with its change of clothes and the backpack of essentials Louise had assembled. There was no point in standing around.

"I am Scottie's daughter," she reminded herself staunchly. "I am a competent, successful engineer. I can do anything I set my mind to."

It became a litany of sorts as she made her way into the fringe of the jungle. The dirt road Carlos had sent her on was little more than a muddy footpath. She bent to step under a low-hanging vine and was slapped in the face by a large flat leaf, then another and another. A huge, hungry mosquito landed on her neck. She smacked at that and snagged her loose-fitting jacket on a twisted branch. When she'd unsnared herself, she dove into her bag for her insect repellent and coated herself liberally.

"I can do anything I set my mind to," she repeated firmly, then with another slap at a persistent mosquito she murmured, "but I don't have to like it."

Just then the darkened sky opened up and rain came down in torrents. With no place to run, she resigned herself to getting drenched. Getting out her compass and checking it frequently, she plodded on as the ground turned into a slick, rust-colored sea of mud.

The fierce but thankfully brief storm stopped as suddenly as it had started. Instead of cooling the air as she'd hoped, the rain merely turned it to steam. Her clothes clung to her in their sodden state, making walking even more uncomfortable.

Two hours later, the pencil-sketched map and compass in hand and the river before her, Cara was convinced she was never going to find Rod Craig. Growing more furious by the minute, she was picking her way cautiously through the undergrowth along the river when a low, rough-as-sandpaper voice halted her in her tracks. She jumped as though an arm had snaked out to twine around her neck.

"Who the hell are you?" The voice came from the direction of the riverbank.

Her head snapped around, scattering dewdrops of perspiration from her brow. She stared directly into the barrel of a gun. Her angry retort died in her throat as she forced her terrified gaze from that lethal-looking weapon and looked up into bold hazel eyes set in a rugged, tanned face. Then her gaze drifted down over bare, nicely muscled shoulders that glistened in the sunlight filtering once again through the trees. Moisture clung to the whorls of dark hair matted across a broad chest. Hastily donned jeans had been zipped but not snapped. She drew in a ragged breath.

So this was Rod Craig. She knew it instinctively and for the first time she had a slight inkling of what her father'd been talking about. Here in the depths of a Mexican rain forest, when her mind should have been focused on business, she felt the sharp stirring of a primitive, very feminine emotion. She suddenly wanted to duck into a shower, wash the dust out of her bedraggled hair, then change into something far sexier than damp, wrinkled khaki. It was not a reaction she cared to share with the man whose angry, distrustful gaze was sweeping over her.

"Are you deaf? I asked you a question."

"I heard you."

"Well? Who are you and what are you doing here?" The gun never wavered. Cara decided to ignore it.

Her blue eyes coolly surveyed the makeshift campsite in back of her, the muddy water behind him and the chickens clucking in the clearing beside the tent. She nodded appreciatively.

"I can understand your fear of strangers. I'm surprised you don't have an alarm system. Maybe even guard dogs. Then again, the gun is probably sufficient."

For a fleeting instant she thought she saw an expression of doubt flicker in his watchful eyes. Finally, he tucked the gun into the waistband of his pants. She decided that was about the friendliest gesture he planned.

"Aren't you going to invite me in?" she suggested cheerfully. "I can promise I won't steal the family silver."

He folded his arms across his chest and stood his ground. It was an impressive stance. On a poster, it would have sold millions.

"I don't think so," he said. "Why don't you just turn around and wander back to your tour group? The boat will probably be setting off soon."

Weariness and exasperation suddenly swept over her, claiming the last of her patience. The man had been waving a gun at her not five minutes ago and she was standing here exchanging chitchat with him. It was time to bring this absurd conversation to the point. She drew herself up to her most businesslike posture.

"Look, Mr. Craig. You are Rod Craig, aren't you?"

His startled expression was answer enough.

"If there are tours in this part of Mexico, I'm unfamiliar with them. I'm Cara Scott, vice president of WHS Engineering."

His gaze narrowed. "Scottie's daughter? I don't believe it. He'd never send you down here."

Cara was irritated by his expression of disbelief. She absolutely refused to dig out her passport to prove her identity. She kept right on, as though he'd never spoken.

"I have come a very long way to see you. I am tired. I am wet. And frankly I would like nothing more than to get back to civilization, but it appears I'm your guest until tomorrow when I told the pilot to pick me up. Hopefully, we can conclude our business before then."

"You told the pilot to pick you up?" he repeated incredulously. "I suppose you paid him in advance."

Thoroughly exasperated now, she glared at him. "I'm not stupid, Mr. Craig. I gave him a deposit. He promised to fly over at noon tomorrow."

"Which is exactly what he will do. He'll fly over. If it's not raining. If he doesn't decide to get drunk. If the plane doesn't fall apart. Are you out of your mind, woman? That airstrip out there isn't Kennedy Airport. It could be weeks before anyone shows up for you."

She swallowed hard. "We made a deal."

Rod gave an exaggerated sigh. "Unless you got it signed in blood and kept his first-born child, I wouldn't count on him sticking to his end of it."

"He'll be back," she insisted with a defiant lift of her chin. She decided not to mention Carlos's desire to see her wed to his exceptionally strong brother.

"I hope for your sake you're right. I'm having enough trouble on this job without worrying about you." He shook his head again. "What the hell was Scottie thinking of letting his little princess come down here?"

She flinched at his sneering use of Scottie's childhood endearment for her. "You won't need to worry about me. I can take care of myself, Mr. Craig. I found you, didn't I? The sooner you fill me in on why your study for the Usumacinta dam project is behind schedule, the sooner I'll be out of your way."

Her regarded her curiously. "Why did Scottie send you? Why not someone else?"

"Oh, for heaven's sake, if you must know, he didn't send me. I decided to come. We've been getting calls from Mexico City asking about the delay. We needed to know what was going on. None of the other engineers was available. If your report had been in on time, I can promise you I wouldn't be here now.''

He didn't seem overly concerned about the reprimand. He ran his fingers through thick, wavy hair. ''I've had more important things to worry about than paperwork.''

''Couldn't you have called?''

He gave a pointed glance around. ''Do you see any phones? Ma Bell hasn't reached out to touch anyone here.''

''Surely you didn't come without a radio.''

''Sabotaged.''

''Then you should have gone back to Palenque.''

''Why? The work was here. If it hadn't been for a few accidents, it would have been done by now.''

Cara frowned. ''What sort of accidents?''

''Nothing to worry your pretty little head over. It'll all be in my report to Scottie.''

Something in her snapped at his patronizing attitude. ''Scottie's in the hospital. I'm here. Tell me.''

Immediate concern registered in those previously cool, distant hazel eyes and warmed them to a degree she wouldn't have thought possible. ''What's Scottie doing in the hospital?''

''A heart attack.''

''Will he be okay? Shouldn't you be there?''

Cara responded to the concern and suddenly felt the need to reassure him. "It was serious, but he's recovering. The nurses may not."

He laughed, his relief obvious. "I'll bet."

She lightened her tone and appealed to his affection for Scottie. "Look, Mr. Craig, I have to report something to my father. If you're having trouble with the study, perhaps I'll be able to help. Let's go inside and talk about it."

Despite her attempt to call a truce, Rod still regarded her with insulting skepticism. Her temper flared, but she knew better than to indulge it. Decisively, she marched past him and into the tent. She looked around for a place to sit, saw only a drawing table, cot and the hammock that hung between two poles. She chose the cot. It was only after she was seated that she realized that Rod hadn't followed her inside.

"Well, damn the man," she said and stalked outside. She was just in time to see him walking toward the river as nonchalantly as if he were out for his evening stroll. Hands jammed in her pockets so she couldn't use them to wring his neck, she went after him.

"Mr. Craig!" she called out.

She'd taken no more than half a dozen indignant steps on the rain-slickened ground when her feet shot out from under her. Unable to stop herself, she slid in the red mud all the way to the water's edge, where she landed unceremoniously at Rod's feet. It was absolutely, positively the last straw. She felt like pounding her fist into the mud. Absurdly, she felt even more like crying.

To add insult to injury, she heard the beginning of a chuckle. She refused, she absolutely refused, to look up. Then suddenly, Rod Craig hooted. He threw back his head and laughed in that uninhibited, purely masculine way that rough, brawling men probably did in the bars of the Old West when confronted with something they considered to be typically feminine foolishness. That laugh unnerved her.

It also infuriated her.

She sat right where she was, covered in mud from head to toe, and stared straight up at him.

Her eyes blazed with fury. His were filled with amusement.

One delicate blond brow arched in indignation as the prelude to an explosion. His laughter died to a grin—a very beguiling grin.

He did not, however, quake in his boots.

Scottie was right, she decided in that instant. The man was definitely trouble.

Chapter Two

Despite his unrestrained mirth, Rod witnessed Cara's inelegant landing and carefully controlled reaction with something surprisingly akin to respect. Apparently she wasn't quite the fragile, helpless creature she'd seemed when she'd first made her bedraggled appearance. For years, Rod had believed her to be nothing more that the pampered daughter of an indulgent father. This had led to his quick judgment. Now he was forced to reassess.

He realized that he'd mistaken weariness for weakness. It was a mistake made easily enough. Cara was, after all, little more than five feet tall, just the size to inspire a fierce protectiveness in a certain sort of man. The discovery that he might be that type of man had irritated him almost as much as her unannounced arrival.

But whether he considered it brave or foolhardy, the fact was she had displayed the impressive ingenuity and stamina necessary to find him. With what he knew required rugged determination, she had made her way over rough, unfamiliar ground to reach the camp. She had reacted with uncommon composure to the gun he'd brandished at her. She had stood up well to his glaring countenance. She had barely flinched at his rudeness.

In fact, he thought with a low chuckle, she'd given every bit as good as she got. If Cara Scott needed protecting, it was only from her own impetuousness.

Reluctantly, he began to admit her resemblance to Scottie. Not that at first glance she looked much like him physically. Scottie was tall and big-boned, a robust man with curling red hair threaded with silver. His daughter looked as though a strong wind would carry her away. But on closer inspection the comparisons were there for anyone who took the time to look.

There was Cara's chin, for instance. With its stubborn thrust, that was Scottie through and through. She hadn't said a single word when she fell, nor had she shed a tear. She was, however, glaring up at him now with a look meant to kill, and that proud chin was held high. Those blue eyes, a shade deeper than her father's, glinted with the same fire. He'd seen it on countless occasions, when Scottie was up against a particularly dim-witted or difficult opponent.

The memories made him smile. Recalling her earlier attempt at a truce, he offered one of his own. He held out a hand. With predictable defiance, she ignored it. She picked herself up with incredible dignity under the circumstances, then stalked off, fully clothed, straight into the river as if it were a perfectly normal thing to do.

Rod watched her graceful submersion in the water with an amazed expression on his face. In that instant he liked Cara Scott more than he'd liked any woman in a very long time. With a divorced bachelor's instinct for self-preservation, he quickly dismissed the feeling.

But he couldn't take his eyes away. When the water was up to her neck, she ducked her head underwater. When she surfaced, her hair was no longer curling damply around her face. It was slicked back in a shimmering blond cap that accented the delicacy of her features. His gaze lingered on the full curve of her lower lip, the arch of golden brows over eyes the color of a brilliant autumn sky, the slender column of her neck.

Then she began stripping off clothes. Rod leaned against a tree and watched with undisguised interest as her jacket was hurled to shore. Her skimpy pink tank top clung revealingly to her breasts. He caught just a glimpse of a jutting nipple before she sank back into water up to her chin. She closed her eyes, a look of sheer sensual pleasure lighting her face. That expression, absolutely innocent of any feminine guile, set off an aching need deep in his gut.

When she opened her eyes and found him staring, the faint smile that had curved her lips instantly became a frown. "Are you just going to stand there gawking?" she snapped.

"Is that an invitation?" he asked in what was meant to be no more than a teasing, audacious inquiry. But instead of wanting to laugh at her look of outrage, he found that his blood surged wickedly as the idea of joining her took hold. Obviously, it had been too damn long since he'd been around a woman, if this little slip of a thing was causing his pulse to race.

Those blue, blue eyes of hers widened and danced with fire. "It is most assuredly not an invitation," she said through clenched teeth. "I was hoping you'd be gentleman enough to leave me alone."

Still lounging where he was, he gave her a lazy smile. "I see you've misjudged me already. I'm no gentleman."

She muttered, "I should have listened to Scottie." Louder, she merely said, "Then bring me a towel. You might as well make yourself useful."

The unexpected display of regal command delighted him. Too bad she wasn't going to be around long enough for him to remind her how to treat the common folks. Not that he would have tried, he told himself nobly. He cared too much about Scottie to get involved with his daughter, even if she was a spoiled brat who would probably benefit from a stern hand.

How many times in the early years of their association had he listened to Scottie talking wistfully about

his *little princess*? She was the reason he'd left the
work he loved to tie himself down in an office. For an
energetic, hard-living man like Scottie, it must have
felt like being trapped in a cage. Yet Rod had never
heard him complain when he'd been saddled with the
full responsibility of a daughter he barely knew, a
daughter already into her irksome teens.

Scottie had never talked about his marriage, but
Rod had always assumed it to be an uneasy alliance.
Why else would a man stay away from home months
on end, dash in for a week or two, then fly off again?
It was the sort of relationship with which Rod was all
too familiar. His own parents had been indifferent to
each other and, most of the time to him, as well. He
recognized the pattern with an expert's eye. He'd followed it himself.

But when Scottie's wife had died after a brief ill-
ness, Scottie had abandoned the fieldwork at which
he excelled and had gone home to rear his child. As
far as Rod knew, he'd never looked back. Well-meant
suggestions about boarding schools had been ignored. Rod wondered if the little spitfire in the river
had any idea exactly how great her father's sacrifice
had been. His resentment toward her on Scottie's behalf returned.

Just look at her now, he thought. She'd taken off
on this irresponsible jaunt when her place was by
Scottie's hospital bed, where she could watch over
him. It was unnatural for a daughter to want to be
anywhere else. To his jaundiced eyes, her sins were
mounting again. He stomped down the idea that

"In my bag."

"Then take them into the tent and put them on," he ordered gruffly. "I'm starting dinner."

He expected her to scamper away still flushed with embarrassment, but she passed him with her head held high, her haughty dignity intact. His body tightened and his blood surged through his veins as he watched the sway of her hips beneath the towel that barely covered her curved buttocks. For a petite woman, her legs were long, longer and far more shapely than he'd realized when they'd been covered in loose-fitting khaki. He swallowed hard and began to build a fire, trying to force his thoughts to less dangerous things.

It didn't work. His gaze kept drifting to the closed flap of the tent as he envisioned the scanty towel falling away from Cara's body. He groaned. What the devil was a healthy man supposed to do when temptation turned up on his doorstep?

"Damn!" If that pilot didn't show up as promised tomorrow and get that woman away from here, he might very well strangle the man himself when he caught up with him. Somehow the prospect of a good, old-fashioned brawl cheered him, and he was whistling tunelessly when Cara emerged from the tent.

He was surprised to see that she was dressed sensibly and not in some stylish idea of appropriate jungle wear. She was even wearing the hiking boots, though he knew they must be miserably uncomfortable since their soaking in the river.

"What can I do to help?" she inquired, her mood pleasant once again. That ability to shift from blazing temper to sunny disposition caught him off-guard. He'd expected her to pout. The fact that she wasn't sulking somehow restored his overall irritation.

"Just stay out of my way," he growled.

"Fine with me. I'll clean up afterward."

She wandered down to the riverbank. He followed her movements with avid fascination, then cursed himself for it. He grabbed a tin of hash, then turned the can opener with jerky, uncoordinated movements. When he'd dumped the contents into his iron skillet, he added seasoning with a heavy hand, then scraped off a layer of pepper in disgust.

"Where's the proposed site?" she called over her shoulder. He almost dropped the pan. Her ability to rattle his composure while remaining utterly cool herself infuriated him. Before he could respond calmly, he had to remind himself that she was expressing professional interest, not just indulging feminine curiosity. For Scottie's sake, he owed her straight answers.

"I've just about settled on a spot about five miles upstream, but—"

She interrupted him. "Perfect. That's not so far. We can go first thing in the morning and I'll still be back in plenty of time to meet Carlos. After dinner I'd like to go over the work you've done up to now."

He gritted his teeth against another irrational stirring of resentment. "Fine."

To his astonishment, dinner passed with a minimum of animosity. Cara chatted with casual ease about the company's work, American politics, theater in New York. In fact, Rod never had to open his mouth for more than an occasional murmur of assent.

Her practiced conversational skill must come from all those high-society parties, he decided. He couldn't imagine Scottie at one of those events, done up in a tuxedo rather than blue jeans. No wonder the man had suffered a heart attack. He'd probably been living on filet mignon and rich French sauces just to keep his elegant daughter happy. What Rod couldn't quite reconcile with that bleak scenario was Cara's apparent enthusiasm for the canned hash he'd prepared for their dinner.

When she'd eaten the last bite, she sat back and sighed contentedly. "That was wonderful."

"That?" he said skeptically, wondering with a touch of irony how his own stomach would stand up to the overdose of spices.

"It reminds me of the way Scottie used to fix it."

"He fixed you a meal of this stuff?"

"More than once," she said, chuckling with real enjoyment at his disbelieving stare. "It's true. Whenever he'd come home from one of his jobs, we'd go on our own 'assignment.' Of course, our backyard was never as exotic as this, and we had a barbecue grill instead of a camp fire, but this was the meal he'd fix. He even overdid the spices just the way you did."

Rod avoided her laughing gaze.

"I loved it," she continued. "It was a special time, just for him and me. It was the only time I felt like part of his life."

Her suddenly wistful tone struck a responsive chord deep inside him. He didn't like this feeling any better than he had any of the others she'd aroused. He'd already predetermined his opinion of Cara Scott as the willful, selfish daughter. That opinion had been shaken once today. He wasn't prepared for the discovery that she might have been hurt by Scottie's wanderings. The image of her as a lonely little girl flashed through his mind and was just as quickly banished.

"Tell me about Scottie," she asked suddenly, deepening the crack in his reserve.

"He's *your* father."

"But there were all those years when he was gone. You knew him better, then, than I did."

He wondered what it had cost her to make that admission, but he couldn't tell from her expression. She was sitting there with legs tucked under her, an elbow propped on one knee, chin in hand. Her hair had dried to a golden halo. Her eyes, in the glow of the camp fire, sparked with genuine interest. She looked like a child anticipating an exciting bedtime story. Increasingly puzzled by her and by his own reactions, Rod found he couldn't deny her.

"What would you like to know?"

"Everything," she said simply.

His heart lurched. Without knowing how he knew, he had a feeling he'd just lost it. He also knew he'd do everything in his power to get it back.

A slow smile, the first genuine one Cara had seen, came over Rod's face. With a sense of amazement, she watched the transformation of his hard features as he sat back and, for the first time since she'd arrived, seemed to relax. She hadn't fully understood the instantaneous tension between them, but she welcomed its disappearance. Rod's forbidding expression faded. The stern line of his lips softened. His body's coiled intensity eased.

"Your father is probably one of the finest engineers I've ever met," he began. There was no denying the admiration in his voice. "I went to the best schools, trained under some of the best instructors, but I didn't learn anything until I'd hooked up with Scottie. He has an uncanny ability to size things up, to work with people. Hell, he put up with me, and I'm not the easiest man to get along with."

Cara bit back a quick retort, and he grinned an acknowledgment of her restraint.

"When it came to work, your father was all business. Nobody slacked off when he was around. He put in sixteen-hour days if that's what it took and he commanded enough respect to get the rest of us to do the same without a murmur of complaint. He never asked us to do a thing he wouldn't do himself."

"He does the same thing now," Cara said, but her comment was made with regret. "I'm convinced that's why he had the heart attack. He never lets up. I was tempted to insist they keep him in intensive care so he couldn't get to a phone. Right before I left I had to snatch a stack of reports out of his hospital room so he'd rest."

She chuckled and confided, "I can hardly wait to hear what happens when he finds out I hid them where that secretary of his won't be able to find them."

A look of complete understanding crossed Rod's face, but he shook his head. "It won't work. Louise has the instincts of a private eye and none of the objectivity where Scottie's concerned. If the files are anywhere in the building, she'll find them for him."

"I'm not that naive. They're not in the building. They're in the back of my linen closet. Not even Louise would break into my apartment."

Rod bestowed a lazy, surprisingly sensual grin on her. "I think you underestimate Scottie's power over her."

"Not a bit. She's crazy in love with him, though he's too blind to see it."

"I rest my case. She will not let a little thing like breaking and entering stand in the way of making Scottie happy."

"Oh, I think she will." She couldn't resist a smug smile.

"You seem awfully confident."

"I am."

"Care to share your technique for keeping Louise in line? I've tried everything, from flattery to candy and roses. She's even immune to outright bribery."

"You obviously missed blackmail. I told her if I discovered those files in Scottie's hands again, I'd tell him how she felt about him." Still delighted with her ingenuity, she chuckled at its success. Louise had been horrified. She'd hidden those feelings for fifteen years.

"Frankly, I'm not sure I won't anyway," she said thoughtfully. "It's about time he woke up and gave her the attention she deserves. Besides, he needs a woman in his life."

That hard expression was back on Rod's face in an instant. "Playing matchmaker, princess? I doubt your father would approve. He's more than capable of finding a woman for himself, if he wants one."

"Were there women when you knew him?" she asked hesitantly, not sure she wanted to know the answer. The man she knew had been a doting father, a loving husband . . . when he was home.

"With a man like your father there will always be women around. He's a charming, virile man. But if you're asking about affairs, the answer is no. In all the years I knew him, as far as I know he was faithful to your mother."

There was something in Rod's voice that bothered her. "You sound as though you disapprove."

"It wasn't for me to approve or disapprove," he said, and this time she recognized the emotion underscoring his comments with absolute certainty. He was angry. Before she could question it, he was on his feet.

"Let's get this cleaned up and go over my notes. It's getting late."

The brief amiable mood was gone and, to Cara's surprise, she was disappointed. On some level, she'd hoped that Rod Craig would help her to understand her father. It would have been a serendipitous side effect of the trip. And at first it had appeared that he would. Now, though, he was shutting her out again, treating her as the outsider she'd always felt herself to be. He'd suddenly made her feel as though she were prying. She shuddered as a familiar loneliness engulfed her.

It took every ounce of determination she possessed to pull herself together and get on with the business at hand. She washed up their few dishes while Rod got his reports and drawings. He lit a lantern in the tent and spread the sketches on the cot.

At first she chafed at his intentionally simplified explanations, but as she asked more detailed questions, his responses became increasingly complex and technical. She was impressed with his thoroughness and told him so. His lips twitched with irritating amusement. He clearly felt he was indulging some crazy whim of hers. She refused to rise to the bait. It would only convince him his patronizing attitude was justified.

"Before we decide on any recommendations, I want to see the site in the morning," she said when he'd finished.

"It's not necessary. You have everything you need right here in front of you." He regarded her coolly. "Unless, of course, you're questioning my competence."

"Of course not. But as long as I'm here, I might as well see everything for myself. You know Scottie will have a thousand questions."

"And the answers will all be in the report."

"Not all of them," she said pointedly.

"What do you mean?"

"You said earlier there were problems. You don't mention them in anything you've written. Don't you think I should see them for myself?"

"There are problems, but not with the site itself. At least not from an engineering point of view."

"Then what is it?"

"It depends on whom you ask."

"I'm asking you."

"Well, for starters, there is a small tribe of Lacandones living in the area. They'd have to be relocated. They've already been forced from pillar to post by the mahogany cutters and immigrants who've been encouraged by the government to move onto the land. Their primitive, isolated way of life has been virtually destroyed by the spreading tentacles of civilization."

"We're in the business of progress, Rod."

"That doesn't mean I always have to like it."

"Is there more?"

"There are some archaeologists who object rather strenuously to the dam."

"Why?"

"It will flood a huge section of the valley south of here."

"So? The government must see the loss of land as a necessary trade-off."

"It's not just land. Mayan ruins will be lost at Yaxchilan. There's no way of knowing how many currently undiscovered sites might also be flooded out."

An image of the spectacular Mayan ruins she'd once seen at Uxmal and Chichen Itza surfaced. "I see," she said, troubled. "The government knows this?"

"I understand formal protests have been made."

Cara sighed. It was a side of the business that nagged at her conscience more than she would have liked. Still, it had nothing to do with WHS. If the Mexicans wanted a dam along the Usumacinta, the company's only responsibility was to advise on feasibility, prepare thorough engineering studies and cost estimates and to oversee construction. The ethical and moral issues involved in the possible destruction of antiquities were best left to others.

"What's your recommendation?"

Rod met her gaze evenly. "That we abandon the project and let the Mexican government deal with its own internal squabbling."

"What! You must be joking. This is a huge contract for us."

"Forget the money for a minute and think about what I've told you. WHS doesn't need this kind of controversy, and you know it. It'll blow up in our faces. Every environmentalist and archaeologist in the world will be on our case if we get involved with the construction of the dam. I'd suggest we turn in the preliminary study, then let the Mexicans hire someone else to do the job, if they insist on going ahead with it. Let some other company deal with the negative public relations."

Cara was astonished. Rod didn't seem the sort of man to avoid controversy. She would have guessed he relished it. She stared at him incredulously. "Just close up shop and walk away? What kind of business call is that?"

"Not everything can be computed in dollars and cents, princess." He shrugged, regarding her disdainfully. "Somehow I'm not surprised you don't realize that."

The cutting remark hurt far more than it should have. She studied him curiously. "You don't like me very much, do you?"

He shrugged. "Is that a job requirement?"

"It would make this particular job a hell of a lot easier."

"I don't even know you."

"Then shouldn't you give me a chance before treating me like I'm an incompetent meddler?"

"Look, Cara," he began impatiently. "I respect your father. He's been very good to me. He's let me go my own way for the past fifteen years without interference. If I told him to walk away from this, he'd do it."

Cara nodded. "Maybe so, but I'm guessing he'd ask a whole lot of questions first."

"Some," he admitted grudgingly.

"Then try to look at this from my point of view. I know nothing about you, Mr. Craig, at least not firsthand. For the moment I'm in charge. Scottie's still too sick for you to go running to him to make the decision. I guess I need twice as much convincing as he would."

"What will it take?"

"Take me to the site. Show me what will be affected. Let me talk to some people around here about it. Then I'll decide."

"I thought you wanted to be out of here tomorrow afternoon."

"I did, but I'll stay as long as it takes to make a fair decision."

His dark eyes narrowed, but he gave a sigh of resignation. "You're Scottie's daughter all right. You've inherited every bit of his stubbornness."

For the first time since she'd arrived, she detected a grudging admiration in his tone. "Then we have a deal?"

He studied her consideringly. "Is it the best one I'm going to get?"

She grinned at him then. "The only one."

He nodded. "We'll leave at daybreak."

Chapter Three

The wild braying jerked Cara from a dreamless sleep, her heart pounding. Instantly her vivid imagination sorted through visions of every untamed jungle creature she'd ever seen or heard. *National Geographic* specials unreeled in her mind. A shudder shook her. None had sounded quite like this.

Whatever it was, it was close. Very close. With her breath caught in her throat, she peered through the shadows toward the opening in the tent—and discovered the ugliest donkey she'd ever seen watching her with malevolent interest. Groaning in disgust, she sank back, closed her eyes and waited for her frantic heartbeat to slow.

A burro, she thought, chagrined. A dumb, nasty-looking donkey. Thank heaven she hadn't screamed. Rod would never have let her live it down.

"You're more effective than any alarm clock," she muttered, giving the animal a disgruntled glare. She guessed from the pale sky that it was barely dawn. Rod would want to leave soon anyway. She should probably be grateful the burro had awakened her. No doubt it was better than being rousted from bed by an irritated Rod. He'd already demonstrated his ineptitude at gentleness.

Cara regarded the donkey warily. "I suppose *you* want to hang around while I get dressed, too."

She stood up and stretched her aching muscles. Rod had insisted she sleep on the cot. He had taken down the hammock and moved it outside for himself. At the time she'd considered it a surprising burst of chivalry. Now she wasn't so sure. It had been the most uncomfortable night she'd ever spent in her life. Even the extra padding of her sleeping bag hadn't cushioned her body adequately. She felt as though she'd slept on rocks. She massaged a couple of the sorest spots, then grimaced as she pulled on her clothes. The incredible mugginess had left them damp. It was like getting into a wet bathing suit.

The donkey brayed again and took a few more steps into the tent. He appeared ready to settle in. Cara approached the disgusting animal with a glint of determination in her eye.

"Enough is enough. Get out of here, you old reprobate."

"I trust you're not talking to me."

Cara jumped at the sound of Rod's voice. As he spoke, he lifted a corner of the tent flap and peered at her. There was a sleepy sensuality in his morning look that promptly stirred her blood. Hazel eyes skimmed over her with leisurely, disconcerting thoroughness.

So, she thought with idle fascination, yesterday's reaction to the man hadn't been the result of fatigue or irritation or any one of the other excuses she'd made. Apparently the gossip was true: Rod Craig most definitely inspired lust. Even in her. How interesting and, in her case, disturbing. He was about as appropriate for her as a sky-diving playboy. Having decided that, with her usual no-nonsense efficiency, she set about ignoring the sensations he aroused.

She offered him a sunny smile. "If the shoe fits."

He scowled at her with mock ferocity. "And here I came to tell you that the coffee's on."

"If you'll take your pal out of here with you, I'll be along in a minute."

Rod shook his head as he swatted the burro's rump, urging him back through the flap. "I can't understand what's gotten into him. He never comes visiting when I'm here alone. It must have something to do with your charming personality."

"Maybe he's taking his cues from you. I noticed you didn't hesitate before poking your head in."

"I knocked. The canvas tends to muffle the sound."

"Very funny. Are you always this cheerful in the morning?" she inquired, welcoming the change in his previously surly demeanor. Perhaps he'd decided to cease armed warfare. There was a certain danger in that, of course. It could make him more attractive and then *wham*, she'd have no defense left against the desire that teased at her senses like the brush of a feather.

"Only when I'm about to waste a day taking the boss's daughter on a sight-seeing tour."

Cara couldn't miss the sour note underlying the glib remark. So much for the truce. Her defenses fell back into place, stronger than ever.

"I'm glad you're looking forward to it," she mocked. "There's just one thing."

"Oh?"

"At the moment I'm not the boss's daughter," she reminded him sweetly. "I'm the boss. Now would you please get that foul-breathed animal out of my tent."

"*Our* tent," he corrected. "And be careful what you say about old Diablo." The warning was accompanied by a worrisome glint of amusement in his eyes.

"Diablo?" She regarded the mangy burro skeptically.

"He's a little on the temperamental side. He's also your transportation."

It was an incredibly effective exit line. Cara almost choked on the vitamin she'd just put in her mouth. She took a quick swallow of bottled water and hurried after Rod.

"What are you talking about? Transportation to where?"

"You want to see the site. Diablo's going to take you."

"I am not getting on that beast."

"Don't you ride?" He made it sound like a challenge.

"Horses. I ride horses." She decided not to mention that awful camel Scottie had insisted she ride to a site outside Cairo. It had been a once-in-a-lifetime experience—she hoped. She could still remember the nip that vile creature had tried to take out of her rear end.

"Besides," she reminded Rod, "I thought we were hiking."

"I am. You'll ride."

She took another long look at Diablo and felt her stomach flip over. "If you can walk, I can."

He surveyed her from head to toe as if determining her stamina, then shrugged. "Suit yourself."

An hour later, Cara decided she might have made just the tiniest miscalculation. The one-hundred-percent cotton shirt, which had promised to be cool, clung to her back. The long, loose pants chosen to protect her legs were plastered to them instead. The safari hat meant to shade her head felt as though it weighed half a ton. The mud sucked at her boots. The energy-sapping heat dragged at her. She was beginning to sincerely regret having left Diablo tethered at camp where he could munch leaves all day.

Rod, on the other hand, looked disgustingly un-
fazed by the temperature, the humidity or the terrain. Cara wanted to punch him.

She tried concentrating on the water instead. The
surface of the river was still and smooth and gray in
the morning light. It captured the reflection of the
surrounding trees as effectively as a mirror. Shrouded
by a pale, silvery mist that was just beginning to lift,
the setting was hauntingly beautiful and mysterious,
unlike anyplace she'd ever seen before.

Then, when she estimated they had gone no more
than a couple of miles farther, they suddenly came
upon an area of destruction. The green undergrowth
gave way to barren land darkened by fire. The towering mahogany trees had been felled, and only
charred stumps remained. She felt as though she'd
stumbled into the aftermath of a particularly violent
war. A chill swept through her.

"What happened?" she asked, a note of horror in
her voice.

"Civilization," Rod said cryptically. "Everyone
wants a piece of it. There's only half the virgin rain
forest now that there was in 1940."

"I don't understand."

"The trees were very valuable. Oil was discovered.
The military claims it needs the area to protect the
border with Guatemala. Now the national power
company comes along and wants to flood huge re-
gions for a whole series of dams."

"But the land, it looks as though it's been through
a forest fire."

"That's one way of describing it. Actually, there's a method of farming used by those who immigrated to this part of Mexico at the urging of the government. It's called slash and burn. They strip a section by burning it off, then use it until the soil is robbed of any nutrients. When they can't grow the vegetables, cotton or tobacco on it any longer, they abandon it and move on. I'm surprised you didn't notice it on the drive from San Cristobal to Palenque."

"I did. I wondered about it then, but I'd assumed there had been some sort of forest fire there. I didn't expect to find the same thing here. The mention of a tropical rain forest conjures up images of unspoiled land with all sorts of lush foliage, not this."

"These people have to eat. They're not concerned about preserving the beauty of their surroundings. They didn't go to agricultural colleges to learn high-tech farming methods. They use the ways of their forefathers. There are those trying to teach them better ways, but it takes time to get the message across."

Cara fell silent. Rod slowed his pace and studied her closely. She caught the expression of concern in his eyes. It surprised her.

"You look as though the heat is getting to you," he said. "How about a break?"

Cara looked around her at the devastation and shivered. She shook her head. "Not here."

He nodded in understanding, and for just an instant the barriers between them seemed to fall away. She detected a sensitivity that lured her as effectively as his physical magnetism.

"We'll go a little farther, then," he said.

As they walked on, Cara wished that Rod would go on talking. The uneasy silence that had sprung up between them at the camp had made the whole morning uncomfortable, but almost every attempt she had made at conversation had been ignored or had been met with curt responses.

"Why did you become on engineer?" she asked when she could bear the silence no longer.

His jaw tightened and for a moment she thought he wouldn't answer. Finally, he said, "I like the challenge. What about you?"

"I wanted to follow in Scottie's footsteps."

"That's not the best reason I've ever heard for choosing a career."

"No," she admitted. "It's not. But it's worked out. I'm actually good at it."

Rod chuckled. "You sound surprised."

"I guess I am. When I was a little girl, everything Scottie did seemed so glamorous and mysterious, so much larger than life and beyond my reach. He was always off in some exotic location. I never understood exactly what he did there, but he obviously loved it a lot." A familiar wistful feeling came over her, and before she realized what she was saying, she confessed, "I guess I thought if I could do the same thing, maybe he would love me."

If she'd expected sympathy or compassion, she'd chosen the wrong man to confide in.

"Your father always loved you," Rod said, that odd angry note back in his voice. "My God, he gave up everything for you."

Cara flinched inwardly, but she didn't pretend to misunderstand. "You mean when my mother died."

"Yes."

Taking a deep breath, she voiced a fear she'd often had. "You sound as though you think it was my fault that Scottie came home."

"Wasn't it?"

Hearing the accusation voiced aloud stirred her defenses. "For heaven's sake, I was fifteen years old. My mother was dead. What should he have done?"

"You could have gone away to school. There were relatives who could have taken you in."

Cara was stunned by the coldness in his voice, the cruel indifference to her feelings. He almost seemed to hate her, and she couldn't imagine why.

"Well?" he persisted. "Weren't there other choices?"

"Okay, I admit it. I suppose I knew I was nothing but a burden to him. There was an aunt who was willing to take me, and there was money enough for boarding school. But he was my father. Don't you think he belonged with me?" she said. Her tone was angry, but the fury couldn't hide a plea for understanding.

All the old feelings of hurt and rejection tore through her. Furiously, she blinked back tears.

Rod appeared unaffected by her vulnerability. "Why? The relationship certainly hadn't seemed to mean much to you up until then."

"How can you say that? I idolized Scottie."

He gave her a look of total disbelief. "Oh, give me a break. What had you or your mother, for that matter, ever done for Scottie? Did you ever really try to understand him? You never once came to the places he worked. He was a lonely man. He missed his family."

Cara stared at Rod, amazed by the statement. What he said was impossible. Surely he couldn't be referring to the man who'd glided in and out her life with nary a backward glance.

"You must be mistaken," she replied stiffly. "He chose to stay away."

"Maybe so. Maybe he felt he was the one who wasn't wanted. All I know for certain is that he missed you. Frankly, it didn't make a damn bit of sense to me. I'd have written the two of you off years before, but not Scottie. He'd read those skimpy letters you wrote with tears in his eyes. He'd read them over and over. The latest one was always tucked in his pocket and the latest picture of you was always up on the bulletin board in his office. No matter where we were, it was the first thing to go up."

His gaze pierced her. "Why the hell didn't you ever come?"

She trembled with outrage at that accusing look. How dare he question her relationship with Scottie? She'd been a child, subject to the whims of two adults, each of whom had apparently been determined to have their own way.

"Dammit, I was a little girl. Was I supposed to hop on a plane and take off to be with a man I didn't even know wanted me? It was *his* choice that we stay behind and make a home for him. Not that he was ever there," she said bitterly. "I can't tell you the birthdays he missed or how many Christmas mornings all I had to remind me of my father was a gift under the tree." She gave him a penetrating look. "Why does this matter so much to you? Scottie was just your boss."

"No," he said softly. "He was the father I never had. Oh, I know he wasn't really old enough to be my father, but he was far, far wiser than the green kid I was. My own father could never spare me the time of day. Scottie talked to me by the hour. We sat around bars together, just passing the time. Hell, we even went fishing together. He was gentle and kind and patient. I hated sitting by and watching what the two of you were doing to him. He didn't deserve it. He had a right to your loyalty and love."

There was so much anguish in his voice that Cara couldn't doubt his sincerity. That pain was hauntingly familiar. It was a reflection of her own. How odd that a man who'd never seemed much of a father to her until she was fifteen had provided exactly that sort of loving guidance for Rod. It did nothing to ease the instinctive jealousy she'd felt for Rod even before they met.

Now, though, a million unanswered questions raged through her mind. What Rod was telling her cast her entire childhood—and her mother's air of martyrdom—in an entirely new light. She and Scottie had made a life for themselves in the dozen years since he'd come home. At first, struggling with her mother's death, she'd been so grateful for his presence she'd avoided asking him why he hadn't come years earlier. Lately it hadn't seemed to matter. She was only just beginning to realize that it had mattered desperately all along, that she hadn't broached the subject because she feared the answers.

"I did love Scottie. As for what you're telling me now, I don't know whose fault it was that things were the way they were between my parents," she said softly, filled with sorrow and an odd sense of relief. With the relief came joy. Rod had given her that. He had given her back an image of her father she'd wanted to believe in. Her father had cared after all. Even then, when he'd been so far away.

"Maybe it was my mother's choice to stay behind," she said finally. "She never said, and neither has Scottie. There was that much loyalty, at least. There were no accusations, no attempts to make me choose sides."

"It must have been a hell of a marriage," Rod said sarcastically.

"It was no marriage at all," Cara admitted. "Not by my standards, either. God knows, I never want one like that. If I commit to someone for the rest of my life then that's exactly what it's going to mean. I want a house with a fireplace, picnics at the beach, Sunday barbecues in the backyard and traditions for every holiday.''

The expression in Rod's eyes softened unexpectedly. For just an instant she sensed that he might reach out to her. Instead, he asked, ''Do you have the man in mind for this idyllic arrangement?''

''Not yet,'' she conceded with a rueful smile, grateful that the emotional conversation was veering off in a new direction. ''Good men are hard to find.''

That wasn't exactly true, she thought. She had met honest, kind men. She had dated men with ambition and wit and intelligence. She had even considered marriage to a man who could have given her everything she'd just described to Rod. But not a one of them had stirred her passions, not a one of them had had Scottie's strength or exuberance. While she didn't consider herself a romantic, she wanted it all. She wasn't willing to settle for a lukewarm marriage that would weather time but stir her blood no more than a pleasant evening stroll.

''What about you?'' she asked Rod. ''Where's the woman in your life?''

''Just one? You do me an injustice.''

The deliberately mocking edge was back in his voice, but this time Cara determined it wasn't going to silence her questions as she was sure he intended.

''Don't you want to settle down someday?''

''I tried it once. It's not for me.''

''You were married,'' she said, surprised. He had the air of a man who'd resist the bonds of marriage to death. There was an independent, untamable quality about him. It hinted of strong passion, but not love. "When?"

"A long time ago, before I came to work for your father."

"What happened?"

"I guess I set out to do what you're doing. I wanted a marriage that would be everything my parents' wasn't. The woman I chose was the exact opposite of my mother. She was sweet and gentle, a real home-body. She did everything she could to create the perfect home. I had the perfect nine-to-five job. It was a disaster. Worse, it was all my fault. I was restless. I didn't like sitting around in the evenings playing bridge or dressing up in a tuxedo to go to the opera. I should have realized that before the wedding. Instead I put her through hell before we had sense enough to call it quits."

Cara was somehow dismayed by his rejection of exactly the kind of life she wanted. It only confirmed his unsuitability. Still, she had to admit to being intrigued, not only by the discovery that Rod had been married, but by the admission that the divorce was his failing. She sensed, though, that now was not the time to pursue it.

"What about since then?"

"I've learned my lesson. I'm not the marrying kind."

"Then the stories are true?" She didn't like the way her heart was thudding dully as she awaited his response.

"Which stories are those?"

"That the world is strewn with women whose hearts you've broken."

"That must be someone else," he told her with a wry expression. "I always leave 'em laughing."

It was a long time before either of them spoke again. Rod appeared lost in thought. Cara was filled with an odd sense of having had her world shaken. Rod's revelations about Scottie made her cherish her father anew, and suddenly she wanted desperately to hear his voice. Instead, it was Rod who spoke, insisting that they take a break.

Cara sank down gratefully on a tree stump at the edge of the river. She drank deeply from the canteen of water she'd filled from the bottles at their camp. Rod unwrapped a chocolate bar and held it out.

"Have a piece."

She shook her head.

"Don't be foolish. This is no time to worry about calories. You'll walk them off."

"I'm not being foolish. I happen to hate chocolate." She pulled a package of raisins and nuts from her pack. "Will this do?"

"Whatever the lady likes."

While Cara ate a handful of the trail mix, Rod prowled restlessly along the river's edge. His expression was intent, and something about it made her uneasy.

"I thought this was supposed to be a break," she called out. He glanced up, startled.

"It is." He sounded distracted. "I'm just looking things over."

"Find anything?"

He hesitated.

"Rod?"

"Maybe."

Cara immediately went to his side. "What?"

He bent down to show her the mashed grass and muddy tracks. "Someone's been here recently."

"Why is that odd? You said there were Lacandones in the area."

He shook his head. "These weren't left here by the Lacandones."

He held out his hand. Two bullet casings rested in his palm. A chill swept down Cara's back.

"I don't like it," he said, his expression grim. "If you're ready, let's finish this inspection and get back to camp. I want you on that plane this afternoon."

She decided to ignore his reference to the plane for the moment. She was anxious to see the site.

"I'm ready," she said, noting that he tucked the casings into his pocket. He was obviously hanging onto them as evidence. But of what?

They reached the site after another half hour of hard walking. As he led her quickly over the area, she was thankful for the detailed information in the previous night's briefing. She could see that his choice for the location for the dam was sound.

"Let me take another look at the map," she said.

He drew it from his back pocket and spread it on a tree stump. "We're right about here," he told her, pointing to a location well south of Palenque. "The flooding would be farther south. Yaxchilan is here. The ruins there are bound to be affected. Bonampak wouldn't be."

"Are there archaeologists in either of those places now?"

"I doubt it. There are some working a relatively new site down in here." He tapped his finger on a dot he'd made farther along the Usumacinta. "They've come from San Cristobal. I had a couple of meetings with them, too, when I first got out here."

"According to the map, there don't appear to be any roads. Can we get there?"

Rod's jaw set. "Cara, I thought I made myself clear. I want you out of here today."

"And I thought I made myself clear. I'm not leaving until I have a complete picture of what will be affected if we agree to build this dam. I'm not going to be scared away just because someone fired a gun a couple of times. It could have happened months ago, even years ago."

"I'm telling you that I'm convinced that someone is very determined that this dam not be built. If I'm right, you're in danger."

"And you're not?"

"I can take care of myself."

"Oh, for heaven's sake, are we going to waste time arguing over male supremacy? I am just as capable of shooting a gun as you are."

He grinned at that. "But do you have one?"

She refused to meet his smug gaze. "Not with me." Her chin lifted stubbornly. "But it doesn't matter, because I am staying."

"You do realize that if I decided to swing you over my shoulder and carry you off to that plane, you would not be able to stop me?"

"I'm aware that you believe that."

His gaze narrowed. "Don't test me."

Cara wisely refrained from letting her lips curve into the challenge of a full-fledged grin. "How do we get to the archaeological site?"

"We'd have to take Diablo," he said with a sly glance in her direction. "There's a dirt road part of the way, but this time of year it's virtually impassable."

Cara ignored the taunt. "Can we go this afternoon?"

"I thought you didn't want to get anywhere near Diablo."

"I may not like the idea, but that doesn't mean I won't do it. Now stop procrastinating. When can we leave?"

Rod scowled and muttered a frustrated oath. "We'll decide after we get back to camp. I want to try to meet that plane you're convinced will be coming back for you. Maybe the pilot will stick around a day or two in case we need to get you out of here in a hurry."

She thought of the greedy glint in Carlos's black eyes. "For the right price, Carlos will probably sell you the plane."

They were almost back at the camp before Cara said anything more. She studied the hard, angry lines of Rod's profile. He was clearly still seething over her decision to stay. At first she'd assumed it was nothing more than damaged pride, irritation over her interference in his work. Now she wasn't so sure. There had seemed to be a note of genuine concern in his voice when they'd argued at the site.

"Rod?"

"Yes."

"Do you really think we're in any danger? We're just a couple of engineers. Why would anyone want to hurt us?"

"We represent change. Maybe they just don't like our looks. Hell, I don't know. But I've had a bad feeling about this project from the day I arrived, and it's not getting any better."

With anyone else she might have written that feeling off to squeamishness, but that was hardly Rod's personality. Nor did he seem an alarmist. If anything, he was the type to understate danger, the sort of man who relished living on the edge, but knew exactly when to back away. For the first time, a feeling of anxiety settled at the base of her spine. Her senses became more alert to every whisper of sound, every movement. She thought she was prepared for anything.

She was wrong. She wasn't ready for the sight of Diablo lying on the ground in a pool of blood, a bullet through his head.

Chapter Four

Rod was sitting by the river wondering why Cara got under his skin so, when her terrified scream shattered the silence. The sound made his blood run cold. Cursing expressively, he drew his gun and charged through the undergrowth in back of his camp. He set off in the direction she had taken when she'd asserted a need for a moment of privacy before going on to the airstrip. For the first time in his life, he hated living under such primitive conditions. If the lack of something as basic as indoor plumbing had put her in danger, he'd never forgive himself. He never should have let her go alone, decorum or no.

He crashed through the bush, his heart thundering in his chest. "Cara! Where the hell are you? Cara!" The fact that there had been no second scream nearly panicked him. The silence was almost as frightening as the bloodcurdling pitch of her first agonized cry.

"Cara!"

"Over here." Though her tear-choked voice was barely above a frightened whisper, relief swept through him when he heard it.

Following the sound of her muffled sobs, he found her standing over Diablo's body. Bile rose in his throat at the sight of the fallen donkey. Pale and trembling, Cara was staring down at it. His hand shaking, he tilted her chin up and looked into stricken eyes.

"Are you okay?" He stroked her cheek, wiping away the tears.

She gave an almost imperceptible nod.

"Don't move. I just want to look around for a minute. Okay?"

Panic flitted across her face, but then she seemed to pull herself together. It was an act of sheer bravado, probably meant as much for herself as for him. "Okay," she murmured.

His heart still hammering, Rod searched the surrounding area quickly, but found nothing else amiss. When he returned, Cara was standing frozen, exactly as he'd left her. An incomparable feeling of protectiveness swept through him as he gently drew her into his arms and turned her head away.

A heavy sigh shuddered through her as she clung to him. The flames of desire sparked to life, startling him with their brightness. He wanted her here and now with a force that rocked him. The emotions that accompanied the desire were less straightforward. Perhaps he was a sucker for vulnerability after all. Or, more likely, for soft breasts, trembling lips and hair that smelled like sunshine. He tried hard to tell himself that he owed it to both of them to sort out the feelings before he made love to her, but right now an examination of his psyche was the last thing on his mind.

"Why?" she murmured, her tears dampening his shirt. "Why would anyone do that?"

She gazed up at him, eyes shimmering, her expression woebegone. Rod's heart constricted painfully. His hands, trembling at the restraint, caressed her back in an innocent touch of comfort.

"It's another warning," he told her. "We have to get you out of here."

To his amazement, she resisted. "No. Absolutely not. I am not going to be frightened away by someone that cowardly."

"Cowardly?"

"Killing a poor defenseless animal is cowardly. I'd like to get my hands on the person who did it. I'd show you just how well I can handle that gun of yours."

"I appreciate your desire to avenge Diablo's death," he said, somehow impressed by the vehement indignation and outrage in her voice. Still, he knew her well enough now to recognize that they were headed for an argument. "I'd rather you used your head and took the hint. This is no place for you to be hanging around."

Reluctantly, he released her, wondering if there would be other opportunities for them to explore this growing awareness between them. Unable to look at her without wanting her, he turned toward the camp. "I'm getting your things and we're going to meet that plane," he stated decisively.

Cara didn't follow. It figured. When he looked back, she was standing right where he'd left her. She visibly dug in her heels. Her eyes flashed dangerous sparks. "I'm not going," she announced.

Rod's patience snapped like a fragile glass figurine. "Dammit, woman, will you stop thinking with your calculator? I don't care how much WHS stands to make on this project, it's not worth dying for. You know damn well Scottie would agree with me. He'd insist you leave, and he'd never forgive me for allowing you to stay."

He thought he saw a flicker of doubt in her eyes, but it was gone before he could be sure.

"Are you staying?" she asked.

"A few more days, just till I wrap things up. If it'll make you feel any better, you can wait for me in Palenque. It should be safe enough there."

She shook her head. "I'm staying. I want to talk to those archaeologists."

"Talk to the archaeologists in Palenque. The arguments will be the same."

"I want to see the ruins," she insisted stubbornly.

Her defiance and apparent lack of fear awed him, even as it exasperated the hell out of him. "Exactly how do you propose we get to them now that Diablo is dead?''

"We'll hike. It'll just take a little longer."

"It will take days, and I'll be damned if I'll waste that kind of time on a fool's mission."

Instantly, her expression turned glacial and her words were edged with ice. "Are you calling me a fool?"

The question was meant to intimidate, and he could imagine that many a man had backed down under that frosty gaze. He matched her scowl for scowl. "If you persist in this crazy idea of trekking off to chat with the archaeologists, yes."

"Fine," she snapped right back at him. "You think it's unnecessary, then you can stay here. I'll go alone."

Taken aback by the glint of determination in her eyes, he simply stared at her. He didn't doubt for one minute that she meant exactly what she said. She *would* go alone. Stubborn pride, if for no other reason, would cause her to stalk out of here, knowing full well that it was risky. The woman was maddening. No wonder Scottie was in the hospital. Twelve years of this would give any man palpitations.

Frustration twisted his insides into knots. If he'd been a lesser man, he might have strangled her on the spot. As it was, the temptation to turn her over his knee was almost too overwhelming to ignore. How had Scottie put up with this rebellious stubbornness?

Suddenly, Rod was struck by the urge to laugh at the image of his boss as the victim of his daughter's temper. Scottie was no victim. Hell, he'd probably encouraged that fiercely stubborn streak. Right now in fact, Scottie was probably sitting in his hospital bed howling with glee as he imagined his beloved Cara down here shaking the daylights out of Rod's equilibrium.

"Your father knew, didn't he?" he muttered, jamming his hands into his pockets and glaring at her.

She regarded him with a puzzled expression. "Knew what?"

"He knew you'd drive me crazy. He's still mad at me for taking him for all that money last time we played poker."

A delighted smile tugged at Cara's lips. He suddenly wanted desperately to kiss that smile away, to plunder her lips until they were swollen and pouting and begging for more. He wanted to leave her so breathless she'd forget all about taking off on her own. My God, she truly was driving him insane!

"I drive you crazy?" she repeated, her eyes lighting up in impish amusement. "How amazing."

"You don't have to sound so thrilled about it."

"Hey, I would have settled for respect, but since you seem to be reluctant to bestow that, I'll take driving you crazy. At least it means you're hearing me."

"Oh, I'm hearing you loud and clear, and I don't like it one bit." His own voice began to rise. With great restraint he lowered it to what he hoped would be a threatening growl. "Now maybe you'd like to listen to me. You will be on that plane this afternoon if I have to tie you to the seat.''

''You and whose army?'' she inquired curiously.

''Dammit, woman!''

''You swear entirely too much.''

He rubbed his head, which was beginning to pound like the very devil. ''Especially since you arrived,'' he conceded. ''Now I am going inside for your things, and I expect you to be ready to leave when I come out.''

He didn't wait for another argument. She could fight him on this all the way to the airstrip, but she was flying out of here today. Sabotaging the radio and ransacking the campsite were nuisances, but shooting Diablo had been the act of someone who was deadly serious.

It took him less than five minutes to throw Cara's few belongings into her overnight case and backpack. When he went outside, she was gone. So was the map.

''Dammit all to hell!'' he bellowed. Then he began to chuckle. He decided he could allow himself to indulge in the brief moment of levity. He knew exactly where Cara was heading, and unless she'd taken along a machete to deal with the undergrowth it would be slow going.

She was quite a woman, he admitted. Anyone who dared to take her on in a fair fight would be in for the surprise of a lifetime. That wicked, proud defiance of hers was a worthy opponent. It was also going to get her in a hell of a fix one of these days, unless someone was around to keep an eye on her. Immediately and infuriatingly recalling her reprimand about his language, he conscientiously deleted the expletive.

It was going to get her into a fix one of these days.

He shook his head in disgust. It didn't sound the same. He'd explain that—and a few other things—to her when he caught up with her.

He didn't have to go far. She'd left a trail a blind man could have tracked. He heard her before he saw her. She was cussing a blue streak as she struggled to free herself from a vine in which she'd somehow gotten entangled.

"Anything I can do?" he offered, smiling broadly.

"Yes, dammit. You can unhook me."

"Tut, tut. Such language."

"Oh, go to—" She caught herself in the nick of time and bit her lip.

"That's better," he said approvingly.

She glowered at him. "Just cut me loose."

"Well, now, I'm not so sure I should do that."

"Rod!" Her furious shout was every bit as loud and commanding as Scottie's. He laughed. Indignation brought spots of color to her cheeks. "Don't you dare laugh at me."

"What are you going to do to stop me?"

"I'll fire you, that's what I'll do. I'll tell my father you were insubordinate. God knows, that's true enough."

He shook his head and watched her wriggle furiously, which only worsened her entanglement. "It won't work. Besides, you can't do that until you get

back to New York. I'd go for a more immediate so-
lution, if I were you."

"Such as?"

"You could kiss me." He watched her carefully as
a deeper shade of pink crept up to stain her cheeks.
Unconsciously, she ran her tongue over her lips. He
swallowed hard.

"Yes," he said thoughtfully, "I'd say a kiss most
definitely would stop me from laughing."

She grew very, very still, waiting. His blood roared
through him. His deliberate provocation had apparently hit the wrong target. He was suddenly the one
who couldn't breathe, who was anticipating that kiss
with heart-stopping excitement.

"I wouldn't kiss you if you were the last man on
earth," she said with an air of desperation as he
moved closer.

"Oh, really," he said softly, freeing a strand of her
hair that was caught on a branch. His fingers lingered on her cheek. Sweet, sweet breath whispered
past his ear in ragged bursts. He reached around her
to cut away the vine that had gotten hooked on her
jacket. The firm swell of her breasts brushed across
his chest with tantalizing familiarity. His hand came
to rest on her hip. He watched the pulse at her throat
throb, saw her swallow hard.

"You're free now," he said in a husky, choked
voice.

Free, Cara thought frantically. Despite what she'd
said, what she'd felt duty-bound to say, she didn't
want to be free. She wanted his mouth on hers. She

wanted his fingers to graze her aching breasts. She wanted things from this man she'd only dreamed about. Passion—lust, she corrected—raged inside her, heating her blood, sending her heartbeat into a frenzied rhythm.

She raised her face, meeting hazel eyes that seemed to have captured all the brilliant green of the jungle around them. She lifted her hand, tentatively running her knuckles along the curve of his jaw. She moistened her dry, suddenly sensitive lips with the tip of her tongue. Rod's groan made her aware of the sensuality of the gesture. Flames seemed to dance in his eyes as he dragged her into a crushing embrace.

He took her mouth with a savage claim of possession. There was no gentleness in the kiss, only demand and urgency and hunger. His heat seared her, branding her his. A riot of intense, shattering sensations soared inside her. This was it, the wild passion she'd craved, the unthinking roar of excitement through her blood. Now that she knew it existed, she could never settle for less.

But it was wrong. Rod was wrong. He was not the man she'd dreamed of, not the one who'd cherish her and keep her safe. Just look at the mess they were in now because of his life-style. He'd be exactly like Scottie, always roaming, always saying goodbye, and she wouldn't be able to bear it. Even now, with her head spinning from the scent of him, the feel of him, she felt the pain of goodbye.

"No!" It was a quiet, desperate plea as she struggled to free herself from the embrace and the emotions.

"Yes." He looked into her eyes, his fingers gentle as they touched her swollen, sensitive lips. "Oh, yes."

Unable to resist, she melted into his kiss, told herself she deserved to experience the exquisite touch just this once. Her arms crept around his shoulders. Her fingers tangled in silken hair as she opened her mouth to the sweet invasion of his tongue. The kiss left her breathless and, God help her, wanting more.

This time, though, it was Rod who ended the embrace, literally lifting her and setting her down a few inches away. Still the heat and hunger leaped between them. He kept his hands at her waist, and his eyes never wavered from hers.

"I want you," he said with unexpected candor. Three words with the power to set off fireworks. A declaration that could change her life forever. His eyes filled with regret.

"But not here and not now."

Cara drew in a ragged breath and fought for composure. Years of practice playing the cool, unflappable businesswoman helped her now. "Not ever," she said without even a hint of a tremor in her voice.

"Not even you are stubborn enough to keep us apart," he said with a touch of arrogance that set her pulse to racing. "Our time will come."

"It can't. Be sensible."

He gave her a rueful smile. "Oh, my dear, I am being incredibly sensible. It's the only thing keeping me from taking you into that tent and making love to you until we're both too tired to even think, though that's exactly what I want to do."

The bold, heartfelt words set her aflame, but they didn't consume the doubts. "But we're all wrong for each other."

"Probably."

His easy acknowledgement of that brought a lump to her throat. A denial, even a halfhearted one, would have been nice. It would have given her hope.

False hope, she reminded herself sternly. "Nothing will ever happen between us," she said with every ounce of conviction she could manage. Her heart actually ached as she said it.

Looking him directly in the eye, she added, "I won't be one of your quick and easy conquests."

The remark struck home. His expression turned hard with a swiftness that startled her. Even so, she almost welcomed this new burst of anger. It was safer by far than the fierce longing that had darkened his eyes only moments ago.

"Don't start judging me."

"If we'd stuck to business, your morals wouldn't be an issue."

"I'm not the only one to blame for the kiss, princess. You enjoyed it every bit as much as I did. That's why I felt I had to warn you before this went any further. I made a decision about my way of life a long time ago. No encumbrances. No responsibilities. You won't change that."

The words were like blows, bringing her back to reality with a crash, but all she said was, "Sounds lonely."

He met her gaze levelly. "If I want company, I can find it easily enough."

He was baiting her with the cruel remark. She knew it, but she rose to it anyway. "And that's the kind of *company* you want? No strings attached. No commitments. Do you even remember their names? Would you remember mine?"

"How could I forget? It's on my paycheck."

Cara drew back her hand to hit him, but he caught her arm in midswing. "Don't even think about it, princess."

"I'm thinking much worse."

"Then it's a good thing I'm stronger than you are, isn't it?"

"Let me go, damn you."

To her surprise, he released his painful grip on her arm. But before she could run or scream—or get in one good punch—he'd grabbed her around the middle like a sack of meal and tossed her over his shoulder. Indignation and humiliation swept through her. She pounded her fists uselessly against his back.

"Put me down, you miserable, macho ogre!"

"Not until you're safely on that plane."

She drew back her foot and tried to angle a well-placed kick, but it missed its mark and drew only a mild grunt.

"Try that again, short stuff, and you'll have a hell of a time sitting down on that plane ride."

Cara froze. "You wouldn't dare."

"Don't tempt me."

There was an undertone in his voice that warned her he wasn't kidding. She sagged against him, letting herself become deadweight. If he was going to behave like an arrogant jerk, she'd make him pay for the right. It was a hot, tiring walk to the airstrip. She was going to make sure he knew just how long that walk was.

The plan, of course, went wildly awry. Apparently, Rod never tired. He was whistling cheerfully the whole way. She wanted to strangle him. And with every step he took she grew increasingly aware of him—his heat, his scent, his strength. She was torn between indignation and the desire to slide down his body until she could feel the brand of every inch of it.

They reached the clearing in far less time than it had taken her to make the same trip coming in. Still, it was nearly two o'clock in the afternoon. She'd told Carlos she would meet him at noon. If Rod was right about the pilot, he wouldn't be waiting. For that matter, according to him, Carlos would never have shown up in the first place.

As they stepped out into the open, where Cara had a clear view of the airstrip, it brought her enormous satisfaction to see that the plane was sitting there, exactly as she'd said it would be. Not that she had any intention of leaving on it, of course.

Before she could even indulge in a few gloating remarks, Rod said, "Well, princess, it looks as though you were right about your pal Carlos."

It took the wind right out of her sails. She couldn't very well lord her superior understanding of human nature over a man who'd already conceded it.

"Do you suppose you could put me down now?" she inquired with great dignity.

"Embarrassed?"

"Let's just say I prefer more conventional modes of transportation."

"In that case, you should be ecstatic to be getting on that plane."

There was no point in explaining to him yet again that she had no intention of being on that plane when it took off. Especially since she heard the engines revving up. Carlos, it appeared, had grown tired of waiting.

Rod heard the same cough and sputter she heard. He took off at a run. Unfortunately—from his point of view—they were behind the plane. Carlos apparently never even saw Rod's frantic race down the airstrip with Cara bouncing over his shoulder. When the plane was in the air and out of sight, the only sounds besides the shriek of birds were Rod's muttered oaths. His range was even more colorful than she'd realized. She tried very hard to suppress a smile.

"I don't suppose you gave him any instructions about what to do if you weren't here today," he said, plunking her unceremoniously on her feet. She wobbled unsteadily and had to grab his arm for support. The already tensed muscle quivered at her touch.

"Afraid not," she said without the slightest display of regret. "I guess you're stuck with me."

"You seem to find this amusing."

"I wouldn't go that far."

"Good, because with Diablo dead there's not a damn thing funny about it. That plane was our only way out of here."

Something in the quiet, ominous tone of his voice frightened her even more effectively than finding the dead donkey had. Her heart lurched. "You mean we really are stuck here?"

"Bingo, princess."

"Not forever," she said, but her bluster was beginning to fail her. Her voice shook. Rod might bear a resemblance to Tarzan, but she was no Jane. This jungle was not her natural habitat and she had no intention of spending the rest of her days in it.

Rod shrugged, showing no mercy. "Who knows? At the moment, I don't have another suitable method of transportation in mind. Do you?"

Something clicked in her brain. Her expression brightened. "Canoe. We could go by canoe."

"Then you'd better get busy carving one out of a tree trunk. I don't have one."

"The Lacandones do. You said so."

"That's nice for them. It doesn't help us."

"You can buy one."

"For a lady who was determined to stay, suddenly you seem awfully anxious to leave."

Something in his voice nagged at her. She looked into his eyes and caught the glint of amusement before he could hide it. Her own gaze narrowed. "We're not in as much trouble as you want me to believe, are we?"

"Oh, we are definitely in danger. Diablo is proof enough of that."

"But we're not stranded?"

He appeared ever-so-slightly guilty. "Not exactly."

"What exactly?"

"I've chartered a plane to come back for me."

She refused to admit to the tiniest smidgen of relief. "What makes you think *your* pilot will come?" she taunted airily.

"He'd better come, or I'll see to it that he's fired. He works for WHS."

She took the announcement in stride. "Then we don't have a problem, do we?"

"Not unless you hoped to be back in New York before the end of the month."

"The end of the month?" she repeated slowly, as his words sank in.

"Yep," he said, turning toward the jungle.

She stared after him. Two more weeks alone with Rod. Two more weeks with some cowardly, trigger-happy maniac stalking them. Her heart thumped uneasily.

Worse, she wasn't exactly sure which prospect disturbed her more.

Chapter Five

By sunset Rod had been worn down by Cara's un-
usually agreeable if slightly silent demeanor. He'd
been waiting for more badgering, but it hadn't come.
Instead, to his complete bafflement, it seemed she'd
all but forgotten about the archaeological site that
had been so all-fired important to her only a few
hours earlier.

She'd taken a solitary swim when they'd returned
to camp, then left her spare set of clothes dangling
provocatively from tree branches to dry. He'd had to
avert his gaze from the lacy bra and skimpy panties to
keep his desire in check. He had the darkest suspicion it was a deliberate taunt, but her reserved behavior had mocked his thoughts.

She had helped with dinner, but said no more than
was necessary, although she had jumped and averted
her eyes each time their hands had brushed acciden-
tally. By the time they'd eaten and settled back with
coffee, his own nerves were stretched so tightly they
would have snapped at the slightest touch. As evening fell, he was forced to bow to her impressive skill
at psychological warfare.

She hadn't pouted or yelled or argued. She knew by
then that he was fully aware of her position about
seeing the archaeologists. She had waited with ex-
traordinary patience for him to capitulate. With a sigh
of resignation, he did, cursing Scottie for having
taught her so well.

"We'll start for the archaeological site in the
morning," he said at last.

She nodded, but didn't gloat. "Thank you."

He shrugged. "For what? You're the boss."

A shadow passed across her blue eyes and her lips
tightened, but again she said nothing.

Not fully understanding why he felt the need, he
did a little intentional goading of his own. "With any
luck Maria Herrera will be there, too." He injected a
warm note of enthusiasm in his voice. It was not entirely feigned. Maria was fascinating. "She often goes
to visit and work as a volunteer."

"Who is she?"

"I suppose you'd describe her as an environmentalist, a bit of a colorful maverick, really. She's well
known in Mexico City. She's been working for the
preservation of the rain forest. She's also a staunch

advocate for the Lacandones and maybe something of an archaeologist as well. She knows more about the Mayans than anyone I've ever met, including the archaeologists working this site. She's an incredible woman."

Cara regarded him shrewdly. "Do you know her well?"

"Well enough." The equivocation was intentional. He had to admit he enjoyed the little gleam of curiosity it aroused in Cara's eyes, the slightly jealous undertone in her voice.

"Where does she live? In Palenque?"

"Yes." He twisted the knife. "You'd like the house, I think. It has a beautiful courtyard, filled with flowers. It's so peaceful there in the evening, when the air is soft and the sunlight is fading. I think it's the first time I've ever seen so many hummingbirds. It's—"

Cara interrupted him. "Tell me about the others who will be there."

He restrained the desire to grin, yawning widely instead. "It's late. Don't you think we should be getting some sleep, if we're going to set out at the crack of dawn?"

"It's barely nine. I don't need that much sleep. Do you?"

This time their eyes met and awareness sizzled between them. One game ended and another began. He swallowed hard and wondered if he could get by on no sleep at all. The tantalizing images that suddenly flashed through his mind assured him of a restless night.

"No," he said, but his voice was choked. Blast the woman! Never before had he had quite so much trouble concentrating. Nor had any woman seemed more appealing by far than work. Even this little jaunt he'd agreed to make was absolute foolishness, something he would never have done for anyone who didn't have big blue eyes, a winning smile and an irritating way of setting his blood on fire when he least expected it.

"Fine," she was saying to him with cheerful innocence. "If you don't have to go to bed now, you might as well tell me about the others. I like to know the people I'm dealing with."

"Actually, I don't know them all that well myself. I met with one of them a couple of times in Palenque and then visited the site once. Rafael Riva is the archaeologist in charge. He's articulate, intelligent and dedicated. The Mayan culture is something of an obsession for him. I think the thought of seeing ruins lost forever makes him physically sick. He mounts an effective argument against the dam, but he's not nearly as hostile as some of the others. At least not openly," he amended, wondering how far Rafael would actually go to save the ruins.

"Does he have a big team there?"

"No. He has an assistant, a young man named Jorge Melendez. I got the feeling he's not all that experienced, but he also seems eager and dedicated. There are a few college students, even a couple of

Americans from one of those vacation explorer programs. That's the whole team.''

"Do you think Riva's opinion is representative of the general view that archaeologists have of the dam, or will I need to talk to the others in Palenque, as well?"

"They vary only by the degree of their outspokenness. Wait till you hear him. You'll understand what I mean. He can discuss both sides of the issue perfectly rationally and still win you over.''

He watched Cara's face as she absorbed this information. From what he'd observed so far, she was an amazingly quick study. He suspected that by morning she would already know exactly how she wanted to approach Riva and that her instincts would be exactly right. It was an impressive skill in a businesswoman. What he knew he hadn't discovered yet was how adept she was at putting those same intuitive skills to work on him. If she could, then she knew that right now he was far more interested in tasting the faint saltiness of her skin, in caressing the satin texture of her bare shoulders than he was in discussing archaeologists, Mayans or this blasted, troublesome Usumacinta dam.

As if she'd read his mind, she lifted her gaze to meet his. The pulse at the base of her throat leaped and an attractive shade of pink stained her ivory cheeks. Her fingers ran through her hair, fighting the tangles, then nervously playing with a curly strand.

"What else can you tell me?" she asked, her voice surprisingly steady.

"Do you really want to talk about this?"

"Yes." Her voice was a frantic plea.

"Why, Cara?"

"Because..." She squared her shoulders. "Because that's what I'm here for."

"And we have a long hike ahead of us tomorrow. You can ask all the questions you want then. But now..." He moved to sit next to her and saw her stiffen.

"Now what?" she asked with a hint of desperation. The panicked look on her face was that of a defendant awaiting the jury's verdict.

He reached out and removed her hand from her hair, then brushed the golden strands away from her face. The pad of his thumb traced the delicate skin under her wide, watchful eyes, swept down her cheek, then lingered on the curve of her lips. Her skin burned beneath his touch. Fire raced through his veins.

His gaze locked with hers in helpless fascination. "You shouldn't have come, you know. Just look at what's happened."

"Let's not talk about that again. You know I had to. Scottie—"

"Scottie needs you there."

"He needed answers."

"He'll worry when you don't show up in a day or so."

A frown creased her brow. "I hadn't thought of that. Isn't there some way to get word to him? Maybe the archaeologists have a radiophone."

"I think they do, actually."

She gave a tiny sigh of relief. "Then there's no problem."

"There is one," he said slowly. He took her hand in his and brushed his lips across the palm. "What are we going to do about tonight?"

She drew her hand away. He could see the tremor of her fingers. "Tonight?" she repeated.

"It's lonely out here in that hammock."

She drew in a deep breath. Then, to his amazement, a faint smile touched her lips. The spark in her eyes teased, dared. "Are you suggesting that you come in or that I come out?"

His heartbeat accelerated at her direct response. He touched the curve of her neck and felt her pulse race. "Whichever you're comfortable with."

Her breath caught in her throat. In an unsteady voice, she said, "Actually, I thought last night's arrangement was suitable." She didn't sound too convincing.

His fingers continued to stroke. "And is that what you want? A suitable arrangement?"

Her expression grew thoughtful. The playful mood seemed to evaporate. "I want an arrangement, as you call it, with potential. This one has none."

Suddenly the conversation had turned serious. Maybe that had been inevitable, but he regretted it deeply. It forced him to admit the seemingly insurmountable differences between them. After a final caress, he dropped his hand from her cheek. "Every relationship has to start somewhere, Cara."

"In bed? That's a risky starting point. People who start there often find there's nothing else to keep the relationship alive."

"But can you imagine a love affair without the passion?"

"No. But don't try playing the which-comes-first game with me, Rod. I don't like the rules."

"What does that mean?"

"That it's a very practiced seduction technique designed to convince a woman that hopping into bed is an acceptable way of getting to know someone. In this day and age that's dangerous. In addition, I think sex—making love—is more important than that and that feelings so strong deserve more respect."

Something about what she was saying struck a raw nerve. "Meaning?"

"That I'm not foolish enough to try to deny that I'm attracted to you, but that makes me want to get to know you, not just to sleep with you. Chemistry is an amazing thing. You should know as well as anyone that after an explosion, there's usually nothing left of value. It's only what you build in its place that has any meaning."

It was a powerful analogy. To his regret, Rod understood exactly what she was saying. He also knew that she was unlikely to be swayed from her principles by something as capricious as her hormones. That complicated things tremendously. He'd been hoping that making love to Cara just once would rid his body of this aching desire, that it would satisfy his curiosity about the woman who'd dared so much just to be here. There would have been no danger to her. He would have protected her from all possible consequences. Now he was faced with several very long days and even longer nights in which to imagine and magnify the ecstasy that was promised in her arms.

He would survive the denial of a physical relationship, though. And the two of them would probably be far better off in the end. He had no interest in another destructive marriage. Even if he did, Cara was not the kind of woman he needed. She was too tied up in her career, too goal-oriented. He'd found that was the ideal woman to date. The demands were few. The immediate rewards in terms of companionship, intelligent conversation, even enthusiastic sex were many. But marriage? No way. He'd watched his own parents go their separate, busy ways for too long to subject himself to that kind of modern-day mockery of commitment.

Even so, he refused to acknowledge that he'd long ago found the more superficial relationships to be boring and unsatisfying. He didn't care to examine the fact that his social life in recent months had been limited to an occasional dinner with a few old and very dear female friends. Like Maria.

Cara, however, had aroused an almost forgotten sense of urgency and yearning in him. It was damned disconcerting, especially now that he knew it was unlikely it would be eased. The frustration made him feel even more cantankerous than usual. If he'd had any of those explosives Cara had used in her analogy, he'd have gone and blown something up just for the exhilaration that accompanied watching it go off.

"I'm going for a walk," he said, abruptly getting to his feet. He needed distance. He needed time to get his rampaging libido under control. A few years just might do it, he thought with a wry grimace. He figured he had the rest of the night at best.

"Would you like company?"

"No."

The brusque response obviously stung. He saw the swift rise of hurt in Cara's eyes, the quick effort to hide it. It wrenched his heart. Still, he walked away.

When he came back much later, calmer, ready to talk, she'd gone to bed. He muttered a harsh oath and searched his backpack for the cigarettes he'd never been able to eliminate entirely from his life. Though he'd technically quit smoking years earlier, he relied on their comfort in tense moments like these and he was never without an emergency pack. He ripped this one open and shook out a cigarette, then lit it and inhaled deeply. The first long drag of smoke burned his throat, his nostrils. The second gave the longed-for satisfaction. He lay back in the hammock, his foot pushing lazily against the ground to keep up a steady, lulling motion. He waited for relaxation to come.

He was still waiting when the first pale light of day crept over the horizon.

Rod was setting a punishing pace. Out of the corner of her eye, Cara observed the grim set of his mouth, the tensed shoulders. He'd definitely gotten up on the wrong side of the hammock. Already he'd growled at her for taking too long to brush her teeth, for wanting two cups of coffee, for asking "too damn many questions," for stopping to tie her shoelaces.

"Do you want me to apologize for living, while I'm at it?" she finally snapped.

That shut him up. It did nothing to improve his mood.

The next time he turned his scowl on her, she grabbed his arm and yanked him to a halt. "Enough!"

He blinked and looked pointedly at her fingers, which were digging into his flesh. She didn't relax her grip one bit.

"What is wrong with you?"

"Nothing."

"Then I'd hate to see you lose your temper."

"Don't push it, Cara."

"Why not? What will you do? Leave me here? Beat me up? How much worse can it get than this awful silent treatment? The only time you've spoken to me all morning is when you're furious about something I've done or haven't done."

"This isn't a pleasure trek. If you'd wanted a vacation tour, you should have signed up for one in Palenque."

She shook her head in disgust. "You really can be a pompous idiot when you want to be, can't you?"

Startled eyes met hers. That was where she saw the first hint of amusement. It was followed by that raucous boom of laughter that made her heart beat unsteadily.

"Okay. You're right," he conceded ruefully. "I have been a real jerk. Planning to fire me?"

She paused thoughtfully. Let him squirm. She glanced at him. He didn't seem especially concerned. If anything, he looked amused. "No," she said reluctantly. "At least not until you get me back to civilization."

"I guess that gives me a little time to get you to change your mind. I promise to be on my best behavior, princess."

It was said with complete sincerity. His gaze was serious now, his eyes filled with good intention. Cara didn't believe a word he said. *Best behavior!* Horse feathers! The man didn't know the meaning of the word.

"I'll settle for a little professionalism."

"You wound me, princess. When it comes to business, I am very professional."

"I'm having a little trouble following this. Do you actually think you've been businesslike this morning?"

"This morning had nothing to do with business."

"Explain."

His eyes glinted dangerously. "Not even you can be that naive."

A slow flush crept up Cara's neck and flooded her face. The sound of her heart beating roared in her ears. "Hasn't any woman ever said no to you before?"

"Not twice in a row," he said, then taunted, "and none of them have meant it."

"Then you've been beating the odds for long enough. It's about time someone put you in your place."

"And is that why you kept me out of your bed last night? To teach me a lesson?"

Cara shook her head. "I kept you out because I didn't want you there."

Liar! A chastising voice was practically screeching in her ear. She was surprised Rod couldn't hear it. Then again, judging from the look of disbelief in his eyes, perhaps he did.

They turned inland the next day. The rain fell relentlessly, hour after hour. By the third day the oppressive heat left Cara feeling as cranky as Rod had been on the day they set out. She was exhausted and too proud to admit it. Her enthusiasm for the meeting had waned sometime during the night when she'd had to sleep sitting up to keep the rain from drowning her.

"How much farther?" she asked, when they stopped to take a break. They'd had a solid fifteen minutes without rain, but the ground was a sea of mud. She plopped down in it anyway. She'd given up worrying about her appearance midway through the first day.

"It shouldn't be more than an hour or so from here."

"How can you tell? This all looks exactly the same to me."

"That's why I'm leading and you're following."

"Thanks for that bit of insight, Davy Crockett."

Rod took a long swallow from his canteen and leaned back against a tree. He closed his eyes and settled his hat over his face.

She glared at him. The man could make himself comfortable on a bed of nails. "Are you going to sleep?"

"I'm resting."

"A little beauty sleep before you see your old friend Maria?" she inquired with perhaps a touch too much sarcasm. He lifted his hat slightly and peered at her with one baleful eye.

"Oh, never mind."

She unknotted the bandanna he'd loaned her and used it to wipe the perspiration from her face. Her hair hung in damp, limp clumps. She absolutely refused to take out a mirror and look at it. No wonder Rod had stopped making passes at her. He probably preferred his women to look as though they'd just stepped off the pages of *Vogue*. She wasn't even clean.

If she ever got out of this godforsaken place, she swore she was going to sit in her apartment with the air conditioner set at sixty degrees for a month. She sighed with pleasure at the prospect.

The following month she was going to sit in a bathtub with bubbles up to her chin until her skin shriveled up like a prune.

She was going to order carry-out Chinese one night and Italian the next until she'd been through every item on the menus of her favorite restaurants.

And she was going to drink champagne. And iced tea. And lemonade. And diet cola. And her special blend of coffee. Correction. *Iced* coffee. There would be ice in everything, including the champagne. Let the French cringe. She wanted everything cold.

She opened her canteen, took a drink of lukewarm water and grimaced. It snapped her back to reality.

That was when she also noticed the movement behind the trees. And saw the still, watchful faces. And the arrows.

Oh, dear God!

Chapter Six

They were surrounded.

Cara was certain an entire army of hostile Mexicans was hidden in the jungle, watching them, waiting for who knew what sign before attacking. Eyes wide and heart racing, she bit back a scream. Every muscle in her body tensed and perspiration trickled down the middle of her back. She was terrified to move for fear every one of those arrows would be aimed directly at her. They probably had poisonous tips, too. Not that they didn't look deadly enough as it was.

"Rod," she whispered, never taking her eyes off of the silent, watchful Mexicans, whose blank expressions seemed increasingly ominous. "Rod, wake up!"

The only response was his deep, steady breathing. She nudged him with her foot.

"So help me, if you don't wake up and deal with this," she swore fervently, "I will borrow one of those arrows and personally put it through your contemptible heart."

"What's the problem, princess?"

There was no sleepy confusion about the response, just straightforward curiosity. In fact, he sounded thoroughly wide-awake. She risked a quick peek in his direction. He looked wide-awake—and unconcerned. She felt like shaking him until those perfect white teeth of his rattled.

"Oh, not much for you to worry about," she said with a nasty edge of sarcasm in her voice. "We're just surrounded by men with bows and arrows. I could be wrong, but they don't seem especially friendly."

He glanced around with no more than cursory interest, shrugged and settled his hat over his eyes. "Don't worry about it."

She scowled at him and this time when she nudged him, it was with an elbow straight to the ribs. "Don't you dare go back to sleep. What do you mean don't worry about it? You haven't really looked. Did you actually even see them? I'm telling you we're about to be robbed or murdered or something." She shuddered at the thought.

He sighed and tilted his hat up. "Princess, quit worrying. I guarantee you there's not much I miss. You can get yourself killed by not staying alert."

"Exactly. So how come you're not panicked now?"

"Why should I panic? They're friendly."

Cara took another disbelieving look. She was met by those unblinking, dark-eyed stares. They only reconfirmed her impression. But she wanted to believe Rod. She really did. She tried taking the statement on faith, but her pulse wasn't buying it.

"What makes you so sure these guys are friendly?"

"Instinct."

"Instinct?" she repeated incredulously. Her heart was hammering and he was perfectly calmly discussing some stupid sixth sense he thought he had. It was maddening, to say nothing of life-threatening. "Do you realize if your instinct had been wrong, we'd be dead right now?"

"But we're not, are we?"

"Oh, go to hell," she snapped in exasperation. It was impossible to dispute that kind of convoluted male logic.

"I'd rather go back to sleep."

"Terrific. Sleep. Would you mind loaning me the gun in the meantime? Just in case your instincts have failed you, of course."

"Princess, I promise you I have not made a mistake. Those are Lacandones. Mensäbäk is not far away, and there are several other settlements scattered around Lake Naja. They know me, by sight anyway. You're the attraction. They don't see many blue-eyed blondes in this part of the jungle."

The concept was not nearly as comforting as Rod had obviously intended it to be. "What if they decide they like having me around?"

He actually had the audacity to chuckle at that. Cara didn't see the humor.

"In that case, I probably would have to use my gun," Rod conceded. "Meantime, just settle back and get some rest."

Since there seemed little else she could do, Cara tried to follow his advice. When no arrows pierced her heart, she actually found herself relaxing, her breathing returning to normal. Then she stopped to consider the situation. If the Lacandones were friendly and if they were likely to be dislocated by the dam, she ought to be talking to them about it, not sitting here letting her imagination run wild.

Cautiously she got to her feet. Again, when nothing happened, when no arrows whizzed past her head, she took a step forward, only to have a hand clamp firmly around her ankle.

"Where the hell do you think you're going?"

"To talk to them."

"Are you out of your mind?"

"You're the one who said they were harmless."

"I said they probably wouldn't kill us. I didn't mean they'd invite you over to have tea. Besides, you can't speak their dialect."

"Rod, this is important. I can work around the language barrier. That dam could wipe out their land. I want to know how they feel about it."

"How do you think they feel? Just because they don't live in bungalows with white picket fences doesn't mean they want to be forced out of their homes every time the government thinks up some new project for this part of Mexico.''

"Thanks for the insight, but I'll feel better if I hear that from them.''

He groaned. "Why the hell couldn't Scottie have insisted you stick to piano lessons and tea parties?''

"Because he wasn't around. By the time he turned up, I was playing drums and hooked on coffee. Now are you going to help me with this or not?''

"You're not going to give it a rest, are you?''

"No.''

He sighed and stood up. "Then let's go. I'm pretty sure these men came from the settlement near the archaeological site. It's not much, just a few huts, but you can see the way they live.''

"We don't need to go there. We can talk to them here.''

"Not anymore.''

Startled, she looked around and realized the Lacandones had literally vanished into the forest.

Rod was right about the distance to their settlement, though. It took them less than a half hour to reach it. There were no more than half a dozen thatched-roof huts. Clay figures were being baked over an open fire, probably to be sold later at the market at the entrance to the ruins in Palenque. The woman who was watching over the fire scampered away when she saw them. Moments later the same five men who had startled Cara earlier emerged and approached them.

The leader appeared to be well past middle age, though it was hard to tell with his weathered skin. His dark hair hung long and untamed. His flat features reflected his Mayan heritage, and his carriage was proud. All the men were barefoot and wore long white tunics made of a coarse fabric that looked as though it would itch horribly in the heat.

"You stay here," Rod instructed and for once Cara didn't argue. "I'll try talking to them and find out if they're willing to meet with you."

As Rod went toward the leader, she began to have second thoughts. Moments later an argument broke out among the men, and one of them stalked off. The others continued to argue as Rod stood by. Dear God, what had she gotten them into this time? She was only trying to do her job, but perhaps, just this once, she should have listened to Rod. They were in the middle of nowhere. They were outnumbered. And from everything that had been going on lately, they were very unpopular with someone. It could be these Lacandones. Her palms began to sweat. There was a prickling sensation along the back of her neck.

And then she heard the music. Vivaldi. *Vivaldi?* Here? Civilization had apparently made further inroads than she'd realized.

When Rod returned, she said, "Do you hear that?"

He seemed more startled by the question than the music. "The Vivaldi?"

She glowered at him. "Exactly."

"One of the boys traded a bow and arrow for a tape player. It's the only tape they have."

"How do you know that?"

He chuckled. "Are you getting just a little spooked again, princess? I'm not omniscient, if that's what you're worried about. I asked."

"Oh."

"Now, come on. Señor Castillo will talk with you."

"What was the argument about?"

"One of the men objected to speaking with an outsider, especially a woman. Señor Castillo and the others overruled him."

Cara wondered if there had been more to the man's objections than he'd voiced in front of Rod. Was it possible that he was the one involved in the sabotage and had no wish to sit down with two people he considered the enemy?

Whatever the truth, there was no hostility from the others. When Cara approached, the leader gestured for her to sit, then began speaking slowly. She was able to understand some of what he said, but she looked to Rod for a translation. He was able to fill in some of the gaps.

"He says that this will not be the first time the government has paid no attention to the Lacandones' wishes. The government tells them go here, go there. It is the way of the world. He says when the government wished to buy the mahogany trees, he tried to explain they were not his to sell. They were put here by the gods, not man. Still, the trees were cut down. People came who did not understand the land. They have destroyed it."

Cara watched the man's eyes as he spoke and saw the sorrow, the resignation. He reminded her of the American Indians, whose lands were lost to a civilization they didn't understand.

"Will he fight?"

Rod asked the question for her, then listened to the response before saying, "He says there would be no point."

"But where will his people go?"

Apparently Señor Castillo sensed her compassion, because for the first time his expressionless face creased with a faint smile.

"He says they will do as they have always done. They will move on to the next place. They are few, their needs are slight, and it is still a big forest."

Suddenly Rod seemed surprised by something the man said. "He asks if you would like to see the land they farm."

Cara nodded with enthusiasm, though she feared another slash-and-burn piece of farmland. "Of course."

Proudly the men led them to land that had been cultivated in tune with the rain forest. Cara's eyes widened at the variety of crops they found. Corn, rice, pineapple, limes, oranges, avocados and tobacco flourished. Here there was no evidence of the destructive slash-and-burn technique. She asked about it.

"That is the way of the newcomers who know nothing of the land," Rod translated. Cara was able to detect the bitterness in the Lacandones's voice.

"He says they have been able to farm the same land over and over because they understand it and respect it. As a result the gods are kind and their harvest is bountiful."

"Tell him I am impressed," Cara said in Spanish, hoping that Señor Castillo would understand enough of the words to hear her enthusiasm.

This time the man's smile was wide. He offered them food before they continued on their journey. Over the meal he told them of the Mayan legends and gods.

"We pray to Hachäkyum to watch over us and heal us. This is the traditional way. We also have Känänk'ash, the Lord of the Forest, and K'ak, the Lord of Fire. Yaxchilan and Palenque are the ceremonial sites of our religion. We continue to make pilgrimages there to show the gods we have not forgotten them, even as the world around us changes."

"But Yaxchilan would be lost if the dam were constructed," Cara said with a sudden feeling of dismay.

"It may make the gods very angry," he responded simply. "Perhaps if we light incense and make foods for the gods, they will understand. We will hear their answers if we listen well to the wind."

It was with the disquieting sense that she might be a party to the further destruction of a gentle way of life that Cara said goodbye.

Señor Castillo looked into her eyes and Cara had the feeling that he could see into her soul. "You will do no harm," he said quietly. "I believe that you are a kindred spirit."

His faith weighed on her. As they prepared to leave, the woman they had seen earlier approached and shyly offered her one of the clay figures.

"Gracias," Cara said, touched by the gesture. *"Es muy bonita."*

Then she noticed the woman staring at the red bandanna knotted around her neck. She took it off and held it out. The woman took it and a smile lit her dark, serious eyes.

"Bonita," she said softly.

As Cara left the camp, she felt the sting of tears in her eyes. It was as if she'd been touched by something pure and gentle, only to discover it was endangered—and by her. Even Rod seemed to have become caught up in the mystical mood. His expression was brooding and he was quiet as they walked toward the archaeological site. Finally he looked down at her. He reached out and took her hand in his and held it tightly.

"Having second thoughts, princess?"

Cara nodded. "How are we ever supposed to know what's right?"

He ran a finger along her cheek. "I think you just have to do what's in your heart."

Cara trembled at his touch. What was in her heart right now was need beyond anything she'd ever known before. She wanted this sometimes sensitive, sometimes impossible man to hold her and teach her everything there was to know about passion. It was as if the visit to the Lacandones had somehow awakened her to the importance of many things, including love. Like the rain forest, love came with no guarantees that it would last forever. It was up to the individual to treasure it and respect the gift while it was his. She raised her face to Rod's, her eyes still shimmering with unshed tears.

"Don't look at me like that," Rod whispered with raw urgency. "Not unless you mean for me to make love to you here and now."

She looked away, but the yearning built inside her, growing more powerful by far than the doubts. "I'm not sure what I want anymore."

The smile he gave her was rueful. "Not exactly the passionate declaration I was hoping for, princess, but you're getting closer."

"That's what I'm afraid of," she said and lapsed into silence.

It was late afternoon when they arrived at the archaeological site. The man who came to greet them was tall and distinguished, with touches of silver in his black hair. If he was disconcerted by their unexpected appearance, he hid it well.

"So, Señor Craig, you are back again," he said enthusiastically. "I thought perhaps your work would be completed by now."

"There have been some delays," Rod told him. "But we will be finished soon. Señorita Scott wished to meet with you to discuss your feelings about the dam before we leave. Cara, this is Rafael Riva. He discovered this site and is in charge of the research."

"Señorita, it is my pleasure," Rafael said, bowing over her hand. She searched his expression for some sign of antipathy, but he seemed sincerely delighted to see them. "I appreciate your willingness to come all this way to talk with us."

Before Cara could respond, there was a whoop of delight from Rod and she turned just in time to see his face light up as he spotted a woman coming toward them. Slender, her midnight black hair flowing down her back, she walked with the regal bearing of a woman who was totally sure of herself. With a thoroughly unfamiliar sick feeling in the pit of her stomach, Cara watched as Rod swept the woman into an exuberant embrace and swung her around. She had no doubts at all that this was Maria Herrera.

"They are old friends," Rafael said in a low voice, apparently reading Cara's sudden attack of insecurity. "Do not seek out trouble where there is none."

She looked into kind eyes that danced with amusement. "You can be so certain?" she said dubiously. "They appear quite fond of each other."

"As they are. But I know Maria well, señorita," he said with conviction. "Her heart lies elsewhere. As for Señor Craig, his eyes light only for you. You have nothing to worry about."

Before she could respond, Rod was bringing Maria over and she found her hand clasped by cool, slender fingers.

"So," Maria said, surveying her knowingly from head to toe. "This is the one. She is very beautiful."

Cara glanced at Rod, who was looking thoroughly uncomfortable. "Don't mind Maria," he advised. "She thinks she sees things."

"Do not make light of my skill, *amigo*," Maria retorted, responding to his teasing. "It is a gift."

"What is it that you think you see?" Cara asked, intrigued.

"A marriage, perhaps. Lovers, surely."

Cara choked. An embarrassed flush sped to her cheeks.

Maria laughed. "Now, let us leave these two men to their talk. You and I will get to know one another. You will share my tent. There is water there, if you wish to clean up a bit. And then we will all have dinner. The others will be here soon."

She bestowed another kiss on Rod's lips, then linked her arm through Cara's and led her away. Cara's head was reeling. She had come here expecting to find a rival. Rod had seen to that with his veiled innuendoes. Instead she had found a willing coconspirator determined to see her in Rod's arms.

When the two women had gone, Rafael regarded Rod seriously. "What are these delays you speak of, *amigo*? They are serious?"

Instinctively trusting the man he knew Maria loved, Rod spoke openly of the incidents of sabotage and terrorism.

"Do you fear I am responsible?" Rafael asked with disconcerting directness.

"I would not like to believe that," he said, searching the older man's face. He did not flinch under the penetrating gaze.

"But you are not certain?"

"I cannot be certain of anything."

Rafael calmly withstood the scrutiny and the doubting words. "You can be sure of this. I have told you my objections to this dam. I think I have made you understand. That is all I can ask. If there are others who threaten you, I assure you it is not with my cooperation."

"Any idea who those others might be?"

Rafael shrugged. "It would be only guesswork. I have no evidence."

Rod wondered how much he really knew and why he was so willing to hide even his suspicions. "Do you think they're simply trying to make a point or do you think they'll actually attack us, if they get the chance?"

Rafael clearly detected the subtle attempt to trap him into a revelation. He smiled and reminded him, "Not knowing who they are, I cannot say, but I am sure you can protect yourself."

"I'm not worried for myself. It's Cara. Her turning up here has been an added complication. If anything happened to her, I'd never be able to forgive myself."

"So, Maria's insight is not so far off the mark after all, is it, *amigo*?" Rafael said with a laugh.

"She is the daughter of an old friend," Rod countered defensively.

"He would disapprove?"

Rod thought about that seriously for the first time. No. Scottie probably would not disapprove. In fact, the sly old fox had probably set it up. "Perhaps not," he admitted.

"But you still fight it?"

Rod gave him a knowing look and dared a more personal comment than their brief acquaintance justified. "As you do, my friend. As you do." After no more than a beat, he inquired pointedly, "When will you marry Maria?"

"So," Rafael said, at once becoming more serious. "This is, how you say, turnabout? Maria and I understand each other. We will find our own way in time."

"Just don't wait too long," Rod urged. "Someday I would like to see you both bouncing babies on your knees when I come to visit."

Rafael's expression hardened. "You look to your own house, *amigo*."

Rod accepted the subtle criticism. "You are right. I have overstepped."

Rafael put a companionable arm across his shoulders. "Only out of concern for Maria. I respect that." He smiled. "But we will talk of this no more tonight."

"Agreed," Rod said. "Tell me, do you have a radiophone here at the camp?"

"Of course."

"Would it be possible for Cara to use it to reach her father? He's been ill and he'll begin worrying if he doesn't hear from her soon."

"Whenever she wishes, but what of your transmitter? Surely you didn't come into the rain forest without one?"

"It was destroyed by vandals my first week out. I haven't been in touch with the office since then. That's what brought Cara flying down here."

"An incredible woman to come to your rescue in this way."

Rod shot him a wry look. "She didn't come to save me, Rafael. She came to wring my neck."

Chapter Seven

Once she'd washed up and changed to her other clothes, Cara felt almost civilized. She was anxious to see Rafael's work and to talk to him and his staff about the dam. She also wanted to hear Maria's views, especially about the Lacandones. Cara had no doubt at all that Maria's opinions would be outspoken and informed. Already Cara had come to respect the other woman's intelligence and sensitivity.

She had a suspicion, for instance, that Maria had read her feelings for Rod on her face, not in the stars. Correctly interpreting the insecurity, just as Rafael had, Maria had then compassionately set about putting her mind at ease. Cara was less sure how Maria had reached her conclusions about Rod's carefully guarded feelings. In both instances, Maria seemed to have insight into emotions that Cara and Rod had not yet acknowledged, even to themselves. All because of the gift, no doubt!

Cara gazed in the mirror, her expression thoughtful as she considered Maria's actions. Running a brush through her damp hair, Cara was still trying to tame the curls and understand the woman when Maria returned to the tent.

"You are ready?" she inquired in her low, musical voice. "I will take you to the work tent. It serves also as our dining room during these days when the heat is too much to permit eating outdoors."

"Couldn't we tour first?"

Maria smiled at her eagerness. "It would offend Rafael. Even here, he enjoys playing the host. Already he has opened a bottle of wine to celebrate your visit. Unfortunately, the meal is not likely to match the wine. We are limited here to foods that will not spoil. I arrived only two days ago, so we do have some cheese and fresh bread and fruit."

"Very continental," Cara said.

"That is good," Maria said with an approving smile. "You look on the bright side always. Your Rod—"

"He is not *my Rod*."

Maria permitted herself a secretive little smile. "As you wish," she said demurely, but with a glimmer of amusement in her dark, mischievous eyes. "Rod has not always had a happy life. He expects the worst of people. A woman with your enthusiasm, your optimism will be able to see that he loses that mistrust."

Wondering how Maria had come to know Rod so well, but never doubting for a minute that she did, Cara listened closely to what Maria said. Suddenly she felt weighted down by yet another burden she wasn't sure she could handle. "I can't take responsibility for his outlook," she protested strenuously.

"Responsibility, no. Only by example, you must show him that not all people are going to hurt him."

"And what if I do? I can't guarantee that I won't ever hurt him." Nor, she thought, could he ever promise not to hurt her. In fact, knowing the life-style he'd chosen and her own dissimilar preferences, she thought it unlikely either of them could avoid pain. She ought to speak up and explain that. For some reason she didn't quite understand, she remained silent.

"It is true," Maria was already saying. "There are no guarantees. But I think the love you feel for him will be enough."

"I don't—"

Maria laughed away the denial before it could be completed. "You protest too much, *mi querida*. We will leave it for now and see what the Fates decide."

They joined the men in the work tent. Despite the simplicity of the meal and the primitive surroundings, Cara felt she had never been to a more enjoyable dinner with more entertaining companions. Their diversity of interests kept the conversation and laughter moving at a brisk pace.

For the first time Cara also recognized the signs of the emotions that held Maria and Rafael captive. The subtle, hooded, sensual glances. The frequent brush of fingers. The provocative repartee. She knew, without a doubt, she was in the company of lovers. Maria and Rafael were soul mates in the deepest sense of the word. Their words and minds might clash, but never their hearts. Why, she wondered, had they never wed? Was there a husband lurking in the shadows? A wife?

She glanced at Rod and saw that he was also watching them with a look of envy. His hazel eyes met hers and lingered. Cara felt as though she couldn't quite catch her breath. Heat washed over her. Suddenly she desperately wanted Rod to reach across the table and close his fingers around hers. She wanted the reassurance, the excitement of his touch with that same need she'd experienced only hours earlier. She heard his sharp intake of breath, saw the swift rise of desire in his eyes, then the careful banking of the flame, the retreat. He looked away and the moment was broken.

Cara felt as though she'd been abandoned at the edge of a precipice. Her heart racing, she was glad when Rafael spoke.

"Rod tells me you wish to speak with your father. You may use our radiophone, if you like. Then we will take our tour. Maria says you are most anxious to visit our ruins."

"Oh, yes. Thank you. That would be perfect." Her excitement at the prospect of speaking to Scottie completely overshadowed her anticipation of exploring the site. It would be wonderful just to hear his voice. Perhaps, if he seemed well enough, she could even ask his advice. She realized anew how very much she'd come to depend on him. For an instant, though, she felt guilty as well. For too many days now her thoughts had been centered on Rod. While she'd missed Scottie and worried about his well-being, he'd suddenly taken second place in her life.

She waited nervously as Rafael put the call through to the hospital. Then Scottie was on the line. Despite the static, his booming voice reassured her that his health was improving daily.

"What the devil's taking so long down there, girl? Are you okay?"

"I'm fine, I promise."

"Then what's happening? I thought you'd be back up here long before now with Rod's scalp as a souvenir."

She heard Rod chuckle behind her and blushed furiously.

"It's taking a little longer than I expected to get all the information. I should be back soon."

"Well, why the hell didn't that scoundrel get his report in on time? Tell him I'm not the pushover I once was. I'll fire him if he doesn't shape up."

Cara laughed. "I think you'd better tell him that yourself."

Still chuckling, Rod took the phone. "Hey, old man, don't threaten me. How come you're lazing around in bed up there and letting a woman come down here to do your job? Don't you know I blew that deadline just because I thought it would bring you running? I've found a few little cantinas you'd like.''

Cara heard her father's hoot. She also heard the note of genuine fondness in Rod's voice and saw the expression of affection in his eyes as he began to talk about the dam. Her own eyes grew misty and she thought in that moment, listening to the easy rapport and respect between the two men, she could forgive at least a dozen incidents of Rod's arrogance.

She also noted that while Rod's summary was thorough on the surface, he avoided mentioning any hint of danger. She was grateful for his discretion. There was no point in having Scottie worrying about the two of them.

''You take good care of my girl,'' Scottie ordered, when Rod had dispensed with the status report on the dam.

''I'll do my best, but she's a trifle independent, Scottie. Couldn't you have done something about that?''

''Giving you a rough time, is she?''

Rod's gaze met hers, held for a heartbeat, then shifted away. ''Something like that.''

''Good for her.''

Something in Scottie's tone evidently bothered Rod. Perhaps it was the hopeful note, the teasing hint of paternal expectation. Whatever it was, Cara could see Rod's immediate withdrawal in the slight tightening of his expression.

"Listen, Scottie," he said in a suddenly brusque, businesslike tone. "I'll have the final report ready for you soon and I'll send it along with Cara."

With his usual single-minded sense of purpose, Scottie persisted. "Why don't you come on up here yourself? You and Cara deserve a little fun after trekking around in the wilds. Must be hot as blazes down there this time of year. Mosquitos must be hell. And, come to think of it, I wouldn't mind a chance to win back a little of that money you stole from me in our last poker game."

That drew a faint smile. "And what if I won again? You'd just have another coronary and your daughter'd see me strung up from some balcony over Park Avenue. She already thinks I'm a bad influence on you."

Silence greeted the bantering remark. "So, that's the way it is, is it?" Scottie replied, sighing softly. There was a puzzling note of regret in his voice.

Rod's knuckles turned white as he tightened his grip on the phone. He avoided the loaded question. "Stay well, old man," he said and handed the phone back to Cara. Then he left the tent as though the flames of hell were lapping at his heels.

She stared after him, confused by the fleeting expression of panic she'd seen on his face. Hurt, anger and an inexplicable excitement warred for control of her emotions.

"Cara! Where the hell are you? Cara!"

She drew in a deep breath and fought to control her rioting senses. "Sorry, Scottie. Now tell me about you. Are you really getting along okay?"

"I'm fit as a fiddle. The doctors have promised to spring me from this place over the weekend as long as there's somebody around to take care of me."

"Oh, Scottie, that's wonderful. I'll come right home," she said before she recalled that she couldn't possibly do that. She was still stranded in this god-forsaken place—and not nearly as torn about it as she should be.

"You'll do no such thing. You stay there until the work's done. Besides..." He hesitated, then coughed. There was no mistaking the odd note of nervousness in his voice. "Besides...um...Louise said she'd stay at the apartment until you got back."

"Why, Scottie, you old devil."

"Stop with the smart mouth, young lady. I'm a sick man. Her virtue's perfectly safe."

"I hope not for long."

"Cara Marie Scott! That's enough from you. I want to know what's happening between you and Rod."

"Nothing's happening, Scottie."

"Why not?"

Cara had to laugh at his bewilderment. "Which one of us do you think is irresistible?"

"Stop with the joking, Cara. This is your old man you're talking to."

"I'm serious. There is nothing happening between Rod Craig and me."

"I don't believe it, unless..." He sounded as though he were working out a particularly perplexing business problem. "You aren't sitting around down there comparing him with me, are you? I know you had a rough time when I was gone all those years, but I thought you'd put that behind you."

Cara was astounded and more than a little dismayed by his perceptiveness. "I have, Scottie. I love you. You know that."

"Then don't make the mistake of throwing away a chance with Rod just because he's behaving the same damn fool way I once did."

"You're assuming he wants me."

"Damn right. He'd be an idiot not to, and one thing Rod Craig is not, is an idiot."

Cara knew if she stayed on the line one minute longer she'd burst into tears. "Thanks for the vote of confidence," she said hurriedly. "I've got to go. You take very good care of yourself. I love you."

"I love you, too, princess."

She stood where she was for several minutes, blinking back tears. When she turned at last, Rod was waiting for her, lounging just inside the tent. Whatever emotion had urged him to flee moments earlier was now under control. If he'd heard what her father said about their relationship, he seemed intent on ignoring it.

"He sounds good," he said.

"Yes, he does."

"Rafael and Maria are waiting. Are you ready?"

Relieved that there would be no soul-searching discussion now, she said, "Absolutely."

Rafael set a brisk pace as they left the camp and reentered the jungle.

"How far is it?" Cara asked.

Maria smiled. "You are there."

Cara looked doubtful. "Here?"

Rafael smiled at her confusion. "We have just begun our work. Where we stand right now, we have found evidence of a small structure. See? Here." He led Cara closer to a mound from which chunks of white rock protruded. It looked no more unusual than any rocky terrain at home.

"This? I don't understand."

"Come closer." He removed some more of the dirt that covered the stone, exposing the beginning of a carving. She ran her fingers over the cool surface, traced what appeared to be a headdress. Suddenly she felt stirrings of wonder and excitement.

"It is stucco, like Palenque," Rafael informed her. "We'd thought it was unique to that ceremonial site, but apparently not. There's also a suggestion of the red paint that they used at Palenque. Perhaps it was the same tribe. We must be exceptionally careful as we work. The stucco is particularly perishable."

"Where are your workers?"

"About five hundred yards from here. We found what we believe to be a temple similar to the Temple of the Inscriptions at Palenque. They are concentrating their efforts on that first."

As they walked on, she heard the low murmur of voices before she spotted the ruin. Here the work had progressed far beyond what she'd already seen. The lower level of an impressive structure was slowly and lovingly being revealed. Above were still the layers of dirt and overgrowth of shrubs that would have made the ruin impossible to spot from the air. Below, though, the white stucco surface was a pattern of intricate designs that she was sure told a story, if one only knew the Mayan language.

One of the men separated himself from the group and came to meet them. Tall and slender, he was an extraordinarily handsome young man, his hair a startling blue-black, his features aristocratic. Even with dirt streaking his clothes and his hair in need of a cut, he had a noble, distinguished bearing combined with a devastating magnetism. Cara could envision him on horseback, racing over the grounds of a huge hacienda, then presiding over cocktails by a sparkling pool.

"My assistant, Jorge Melendez," Rafael said. "This is Señorita Scott, and of course you remember Señor Craig."

"Of course," Jorge said, smiling at them. "We are pleased you have come to see our work. May I show you around? Words cannot do this justice. You must see for yourself. You have come at the best time. Sunset bathes this in golden shadows."

The offer and the hand held out to Cara drew a sharp glance from Rod, but Cara accepted both at once, drawn in by the young man's enthusiasm. He led her closer, warning her to watch her footing. He introduced her to the half dozen other workers, all of whom were eager to explain what they were doing and, in the case of the three Americans, why they had joined the expedition.

Cara was quickly caught up in the feeling of magic that surrounded their efforts. In a softly accented voice, Jorge wove deft images of the past until she could imagine the temple as it once was, the center for religious expression, part of a rich culture just as the Lacandones had described to her.

"You would like to help, perhaps?" Jorge suggested.

"May I?"

"Of course." He demonstrated how they were clearing away the years of dirt that had accumulated, then left her to work on a small sector. It was slow, tedious work, yet the reward of discovery was unlike anything she'd ever before experienced.

"Having fun?" Rod inquired, breaking her concentration.

When she looked up, he brushed a smudge of dirt from the tip of her nose. His fingers lingered on her cheek. She reached up and held his hand in place as she tried to explain the feelings that were soaring through her.

"It's..." She searched for a word that was adequate to describe the emotions. "Magnificent. I feel as though I'm able to touch the beginning of time."

"Then you can see why Rafael and the others can't bear the thought of all this being lost."

Cara knew what he was doing, and she tried to resist. Despite the powerful emotional tug of the experience, when it came to the dam, she needed to think
with her head, not her heart.

"The relics could be salvaged," she suggested.
"The Museum of Anthropology in Mexico City could
create a new exhibit."

"Of an entire temple?" he said skeptically. "Besides, a few months ago, no one even knew this site
existed. With the dam, it would never have been discovered. There may be countless others just like it,
buried by time, just waiting for some intrepid explorer to unearth them."

"But we have to weigh that against the merits of the
dam."

"I've done that," he said.

"And you believe the dam project should be abandoned."

"Yes. But don't listen just to me. Talk to Rafael
and Jorge tonight. I guarantee you that their arguments will affect you as deeply as they did me."

"And Maria?"

He grinned at her. "She has her own powers of
persuasion, yes."

Cara asked the question that had been on her mind
ever since lunch. "Why do you think she and Rafael
haven't married? They're obviously very much in
love."

"I don't know. I've often wondered the same thing.
I even tried to discuss it with him earlier, but he
steered the conversation right back around to you and

NO COST! NO OBLIGATION TO BUY! NO PURCHASE NECESSARY!

PLAY "LUCKY 7" AND GET AS MANY AS SIX FREE GIFTS...

HOW TO PLAY:

1. With a coin, carefully scratch off the silver box at the right. This makes you eligible to receive one or more free books, and possibly other gifts, depending on what is revealed beneath the scratch-off area.

2. You'll receive brand-new Silhouette Special Edition® novels. When you return this card, we'll send you the books and gifts you qualify for *absolutely free*!

3. Unless you tell us otherwise, every month we'll send you 6 additional novels to read and enjoy. If you decide to keep them, you'll pay only $2.49* per book—that's 26¢ less per book than the cover price! There is *no* charge for shipping and handling. There are no hidden extras.

4. When you subscribe to Silhouette Books, we'll also send you additional free gifts from time to time, as well as our newsletter.

5. You must be completely satisfied. You may cancel at any time simply by writing ''cancel'' on your statement or returning a shipment of books to us at our cost.

*Terms and prices subject to change without notice.

You'll love your elegant bracelet watch—
this classic LCD Quartz Watch is a perfect
expression of your style and good taste—
and it is yours FREE as an added thanks for
giving our Reader Service a try.

PLAY "LUCKY 7"

Just scratch off the silver box with a coin.
Then check below to see which gifts you get.

YES! I have scratched off the silver box. Please send me all the
gifts for which I qualify. I understand I am under no obligation
to purchase any books, as explained on the opposite page.

235 CIS R1XY

NAME

ADDRESS   APT

CITY   STATE   ZIP

7	7	7	WORTH FOUR FREE BOOKS. FREE BRACELET WATCH AND MYSTERY BONUS
🍒	🍒	🍒	WORTH FOUR FREE BOOKS AND MYSTERY BONUS
🔵	🔵	🔵	WORTH FOUR FREE BOOKS
🔔	🔔	🍒	WORTH TWO FREE BOOKS

DETACH AND MAIL CARD TODAY

DETACH AND MAIL CARD TODAY

BUSINESS REPLY CARD

First Class   Permit No. 717   Buffalo, NY

Postage will be paid by addressee

SILHOUETTE BOOKS®
901 Fuhrmann Blvd.,
P.O. Box 1867
Buffalo, NY 14240-9952

NO POSTAGE
NECESSARY
IF MAILED
IN THE
UNITED STATES

me. Since I didn't have any answers for him either, I saw the wisdom in dropping the subject."

The unexpected twist in his response silenced her. There was a wry note in his voice, as if he found it amusing that their own relationship was subject to speculation. After the tension his discussion with Scottie had created, she was surprised by his nonchalant attitude.

All at once she found the lack of clarity irritating. It should have been simple enough. She was vice president of WHS Engineering. Rod was an employee. But somewhere along the line, that clear-cut description of their relationship had become complicated. Despite Maria's interpretation of the chemistry between them, and despite Scottie's hopes, Cara refused to acknowledge the possibility that it went any deeper. She began to understand Rod's dilemma in talking to Rafael. He obviously was no more willing to put love into the equation than she was. Oddly, his reluctance hurt more than she would have liked.

Suddenly her enthusiasm for digging to reveal yet another Mayan carving waned. She jumped to her feet and took off, leaving Rod staring after her.

"Cara! Where the devil do you think you're going now?" He ran to catch up with her. She tried very hard to ignore him. He put a restraining hand on her arm. She shook it off.

"Leave me alone."

"You're upset. Why?"

"I am not upset."

"You could have fooled me."

"I am just going for a walk. All of a sudden I felt the need to get some exercise."

"We've been walking for days."

"Exactly. I've gotten used to it. I can't take sitting still anymore."

"I see. I don't suppose this aversion to sitting still has anything to do with what we were talking about."

"I can't imagine what you mean."

This time when he reached for her, he made sure she didn't get away. One arm went around her waist, lifting her against him. His other hand tilted her chin until she was forced to look into his eyes.

"I'm sorry," he said softly.

She closed her eyes, unable to bear the pity she thought she read in his expression. "You don't owe me any apologies." To her fury, her voice trembled.

"Look at me."

Stubbornly, she kept her head averted, her eyes clamped shut.

She felt a sigh shudder through his body. His heat, his sharp masculine scent surrounded her, lured her. Pressed against the hard planes of his body, she felt herself going weak with longing. She fought the sensations, fought to keep her muscles tense, resistant.

"Dammit, Cara," he said, giving her an impatient shake. "I didn't mean to imply that there's nothing between us. We both know there is. Did you want me to have that conversation with Rafael or Scottie, for that matter, before you and I could have it, before we could figure out for ourselves what's happening between us?"

She dared to open her eyes then. His face reflected all the tension and frustration and desire she was feeling. She stopped fighting him then and lifted her hand to caress his cheek.

"Ah, hell, Cara," he muttered and lowered his lips to capture hers. There was hunger and anger and confusion in that kiss. It began with such urgency, his lips marauding, hot and moist in their claim. Then, for just an instant, they stilled, and in that timeless moment, Cara waited, breathless, for his retreat.

"Rod," she murmured finally and with a groan his mouth closed over hers once again, his tongue invading, tasting, dueling in a wickedly sensuous assault.

Her breasts strained against the cotton of her tank top, the nipples hard and sensitive. When Rod's hand curved over the fullness, pleasure spiraled through her. His fingers caressed and teased, increasing the aching emptiness inside her. She wanted to urge his hands lower, wanted that touch to sweep over her belly until it reached the heated core of her. She wanted the sweet torment to swell until it filled her, then exploded in ecstasy. She wanted more than she could have—more than he was offering.

With a sigh of regret, she stilled his touch, though she didn't try to leave his embrace. That would have been asking too much.

"This won't solve anything."

"Oh, I can think of at least one thing it would solve," he said dryly, but he didn't fight her. He brushed the hair back from her face with a tenderness that surprised her and intrigued her more than ever.

"I think we'd better avoid situations like this," she said.

"Which situations are those?"

"Being alone together."

His booming laughter mocked her. "Exactly how do you propose we do that? Take a chaperon back to my camp with us?"

"Actually, that's not a bad idea." The words came out in a rush. "If we had help, you could finish up your work sooner."

"Then what do we do while we wait for the plane to arrive?"

"We could call the pilot from here and ask him to pick us up earlier."

"Okay."

Startled and possibly even disappointed by the swift agreement, she just stared at him. "Okay? That's it?"

"I'm agreeing with you. What more do you want?"

"I expected a fight."

"Why waste the energy, when we both know you're right? At least about calling the pilot."

"And the help?"

"Not such a good idea. We still don't know if any of the people here are involved in what's been happening. The last thing we need to do is invite the wolf into the chicken coop."

As if to prove his point, a shot rang out. Cara screamed as the bullet whizzed past her head. A second shot split the air. Then Rod's body was on hers and she was falling, face first, into the mud.

Chapter Eight

Cara was suffocating.

Rod's deadweight—an all-too-fitting description that almost gagged her with its implications—had her pinned to the ground, her face buried in oozing, breath-defying mud. The fear of blacking out swept through her mind. Even more horrifying than her own plight was the thought that Rod had actually been killed by that second shot. He hadn't moved so much as a muscle since they'd hit the ground.

Damn him! she thought furiously. He'd better not be dead. They had too much yet to resolve. If he took the easy way out, she was going to kill him. The irrational thought sent a hysterical giggle through her, then snapped her back to reality.

She fought to lift her head, so she could gasp for enough air to think clearly. She had to make some decisions right now, and they had to be the right ones. Would the shots have drawn the attention of the others in the camp? Or had someone there actually fired them? Was help on the way? Or was the would-be killer closing in? The questions careened through her mind without slowing long enough for answers to form. What should she do? Just for an instant she wished Rod were in command, even ordering her around.

But he wasn't. She couldn't even tell if he was breathing. He still hadn't uttered a sound, not so much as a moan. An awful, empty loneliness engulfed her as she thought of what her life had been like before Rod, what it might become again if he . . . No, she wouldn't think like that. He was alive. He had to be.

In that moment, with absolute clarity, she knew she loved him. Against all odds, against all reason, she loved him and needed him in a way she'd never expected to want any man. They might not have a future together, but if there was a chance, any chance, that he could be saved, she had to see that he had that chance.

Sheer desperation gave her the strength to try to struggle from beneath him, to risk exposing herself to this unseen, unknown enemy.

"Would you hold still?" Now he did groan as she finally wriggled free. It was the most wonderful sound she'd ever heard. The disgruntled note in his voice slid past without registering.

"Oh, thank God," she murmured with heartfelt emotion. Joy surged through her as she sat up, touching his cheek, then ran her hand down his back, needing to feel the reassuring warmth of his flesh.

"You're alive," she breathed reverently. "I was so scared."

"Of course I'm alive," he said impatiently. "Now, would you shut up for a minute until I can figure out what the hell is going on."

Stung, Cara sat back on her heels and stared at him. He did not appear suitably impressed with her relief on his behalf. She decided that the emotion she had characterized only moments ago as love must have been insanity.

"Well, I'm sorry I was so worried about you," she snapped indignantly. She tried to get to her feet, but he pinned her right where she was.

"Cara!" His voice rose ominously and she bit back another angry retort. The prospect of killing him herself loomed once again. It didn't help that she knew he was being sensible and that she was being dangerously impetuous. Granted, only moments ago she'd been longing for just one direct order, but it seemed that domineering attitude of his would always set her teeth on edge. Just once, couldn't the man give her credit for having a brain?

Perhaps he would, if you'd use it, a little voice nagged.

Suddenly there was the sound of people crashing through the brush, calling out their names. Rafael and Jorge were in front, but Maria and the others were not far behind.

"Madre de Dios," Maria murmured as she ran to them. She bent to wipe the mud from Cara's face, then went to Rod. "You are hurt?"

It didn't improve Cara's mood to realize that she'd never ascertained the answer to that question herself. She'd assumed from his foul temper that he couldn't possibly be seriously injured. Maria's concern nagged at her conscience as she waited for him to answer.

Rod gingerly lifted himself to a sitting position and touched his temple, where there was a bloody scrape. "Nothing that an ice pack wouldn't cure. I hit my head when I jumped to knock Cara to the ground."

"What happened?" Rafael asked.

"Someone fired a couple of shots at us."

Now that the incident appeared over, hearing the words actually spoken aloud set off a wild trembling inside Cara. Someone had actually aimed a gun at them and fired it. It was too late for fear, but not for fury. She set aside her irritation with Rod . . . for the moment. A fine rage began to build inside her, along with a renewed determination to discover who was behind this campaign to frighten them away from the Usumacinta dam project.

Expecting outrage from the others if only to cast aside suspicions of guilt, Cara was amazed to see that Rafael appeared dubious about the entire incident. "Are you sure these shots were meant for you, *amigo*? It could have been a hunter elsewhere in the forest. Sounds play tricks on you here."

"I didn't imagine the breeze of that bullet as it flew past my ear," Cara said with a shudder. "You must have heard the shots, too, and realized they were close. You came running quickly enough."

Jorge and Rafael exchanged glances. *"Si,"* Jorge admitted reluctantly. "We heard them."

"So, there is no denying it, then," Rafael said. "These attacks are getting more serious. Perhaps it is time to end your work here."

The suggestion came as no surprise. But suspicious now of everyone, Cara wondered at its motivation. She studied Rafael's expression, but could read nothing more than concern in his eyes.

"I think it's time to have a talk with those Lacandones—" Jorge began, only to be cut off by Maria.

"I can't believe you're suggesting for one minute that they're involved in this," she snapped. "Just because you and Juan Castillo once fought over land and he won."

"With *your* help," Jorge countered. "I know you're their staunchest supporter, but even you can't ignore their history of violence."

When Rafael appeared ready to intercede, Maria waved him away. Hands on hips, she faced Jorge. "There hasn't been an incident in years, and you know perfectly well most involved feuds or wife stealing in the southern tribes. Even they didn't attack outsiders."

Maria's eyes blazed, and Jorge finally backed down. "You're the expert," he muttered, though it didn't sound complimentary the way he said it.

Now Rafael did step in. "Enough. Our guests are injured. It is no time to indulge in old arguments." He turned to Rod. "What will you do?"

"We will leave in the morning."

"Perhaps one of us should join them for the trip back," Jorge suggested. "It would, how do you say, even the odds."

"Thanks," Rod said. "But it's not necessary. If I can use your radiophone, I will make arrangements for us to leave the survey area a day or so after we arrive back there. In the meantime, I think whoever shot at us meant it only as another warning. If they know we're leaving soon, there shouldn't be any more attacks."

"Can you be so sure?" Rafael inquired. "If they seek to stop the building of the dam, they will not wish to see you leave at all."

Cara swallowed hard, but Rod was adamant. "We'll be fine."

Jorge apparently sensed Cara's nervousness and appealed to it. "And you, señorita? How do you feel about returning alone? Would you prefer to stay here with us, where it is safer?"

Before she could respond, Rod said, "She stays with me." Cara saw the hard expression on his face and refrained from contradicting him.

At the immediate bristling of masculine egos, this time it was Maria who stepped in as mediator. She suggested they go back to the camp. "I want to look more closely at your injury," she told Rod. "I am sure Cara could use some tea to calm her, as well. She is—what is the expression?—pale as a ghost."

"I'm fine," Cara argued moments later, when Maria insisted on taking her to their tent and bringing her a cup of tea that had been sweetened with so much sugar it tasted like syrup. "I need to be with Rod."

"You need to rest. His head is hard," she said with an attempt at wry humor. "He will be fine."

Cara wasn't worried about his head. It was like a rock. "There are decisions to be made."

"And he will make them."

"Maria, you don't understand. I'm the one who should be making them. This dam project is my company's problem."

Maria threw up her hands in defeat. "Go, then. He is in the work tent, I believe."

Cara found Rod with Jorge and Rafael. He was on the radiophone to Comitan trying to reach the pilot who worked for WHS Engineering. When he got through at last, he issued terse instructions. The pilot said little beyond acknowledgment of the orders to fly in to the airstrip in four days. Cara was surprised at the tight schedule. It would take them three days to return to camp, leaving only one to wrap up the project. If there was so little left to do, why couldn't they simply abandon the equipment and leave from here? She knew better, though, than to ask Rod to explain while Rafael and Jorge were present.

With the immediate situation calmer now and tempers cooled, they spent an almost relaxing evening with the archaeologists and volunteers. Rafael and Jorge reiterated their objections to the dam. Ignoring Jorge's disparaging looks, Maria gave an impassioned plea not only on behalf of the Lacandones, but of the rain forest itself.

"There has been so much destruction already," she explained with the air of a fighter who is weary of the battle but not yet resigned to losing. Her eyes blazed with anger. "The ecological balance is imperiled. You have heard, perhaps, of the greenhouse effect. The earth already suffers from it. Last summer's high temperatures and drought were symptoms."

Cara recalled the devastating impact of the heat and lack of rain the previous year across the Midwest and into the Northeast. "You think this greenhouse effect is related to what's happening here?"

"Almost certainly. Pollution is only one cause. Combined with this destruction—" She raised her hands in a helpless gesture. "If the destruction goes on, not just here, but in other places where rain forests are treated with similarly wanton disregard, there will be increasingly serious droughts. Rivers will dry up and vanish. Crops will continue to shrivel and die. The long-range implications are far-reaching, yet mankind is traditionally shortsighted.

"The mahogany is valuable. Take it," she said with a snap of her fingers. "There could be oil. Explore for it. The land could pacify the peasants. Bring them in, let them settle it. It goes on and on. Thousands and thousands of acres of untouched rain forest only a few decades ago, and now there is less than half that.''

There was an ominous chill to Maria's words that affected Cara as deeply as anything else she'd heard. Before the final decision was made about WHS involvement, she needed to speak with other environmental experts. Scottie, with his hard-nosed business acumen, would call it a waste of time, but she knew she could never live with herself if she involved the company in something potentially so destructive.

Hours later, unable to sleep, she slipped from her cot. On the way out of the tent, she noticed that Maria was not in bed, either. Perhaps, she thought with a smile, Maria was spending the night with Rafael.

Once outside in the still night air, Cara heard the soft murmur of voices coming from the direction of the work tent. Walking that way, she recognized the soft cadence of Maria's voice, then Rafael's.

"Do you think we have convinced them?" he asked.

"We have done all we can, *querido*. Cara is frightened. I think she will be most anxious to leave Mexico.''

"And what of your friend Rod?"

"He will go where she goes," Maria said with a low laugh.

"I hope you're right. I don't like the violence."

"Nor do I. But if it serves our purpose."

"I still don't like it. What if they are killed? Could you live with that?"

Cara's heart stood still.

"Ah, *querido*, you worry too much. Let us concentrate on more pleasurable things for what is left of the night."

Cara backed slowly away, afraid to take her eyes from the entrance to the tent for fear Maria and Rafael would emerge and discover her. When a hand clamped itself over her mouth, a scream began somewhere in the pit of her stomach. Against that effective silencer, it came out as no more than a soft yelp. Perspiration broke out across her brow as she was dragged into the brush.

She drew her arm forward and rammed the elbow back until it met with rock-solid flesh. There was a mild grunt, but the hand across her mouth never even twitched. She kicked backward, hoping to make contact with a shin. When that, too, missed the target, she brought her booted foot up, then stomped down on what she hoped would be a bare foot.

"Enough!" an all-too-familiar voice hissed in her ear. "Are you trying to let everybody in camp know we're out here?"

Rod released her then and she whirled around. "As a matter of fact, that's exactly what I was doing, you idiot! I thought I was being kidnapped."

He grinned at her, and her ridiculous heart flipped over. "Sorry," he said, but the grin belied the apology. He didn't appear one bit contrite about taking ten years off her life. "What are you doing skulking around out here?"

"I wasn't skulking. I couldn't sleep. I came out for some air. You ought to be damned thankful I did. I just overheard a conversation between Maria and Rafael that implicates them in everything that's been happening."

Rod sighed, the expression on his face tired and disillusioned. "I know. I heard it, too. Frankly, I can't believe it. I would have trusted those two with my life."

Cara suddenly recalled Maria's comments to her earlier about how often Rod had been disappointed by those he'd trusted. How odd that a woman who recognized that and seemed to care about it would become a traitor herself. Perhaps she felt she owed a greater loyalty to her cause.

"I'm sorry," Cara told Rod gently. "I know how much you like Maria."

"Of all people, I should know that people are not always what they seem."

Cara could think of no way to contradict him, not in light of what had just happened. She understood his bitterness all too well. "How did you happen to be out here?" she asked instead.

"I was going to use the radiophone. I wanted to call the pilot and change our arrangements."

Cara nodded in sudden understanding. "So that's it. You planned all along to make a change. I wondered why you'd been so open about the plans earlier. You wanted them to know what we were doing."

"Exactly. I was hoping to set a trap and see who fell into it."

"You can still do that."

He shrugged. "There appears to be no need. If Rafael and Maria are satisfied that they've accomplished their goal, they will feel no further need to attack us."

"What if it isn't them? You heard Rafael. He's worried someone will kill us. Apparently he's not the one in control."

Rod stared at her. "You could be right. I must not be thinking clearly. I hadn't even stopped to consider that," he conceded at last. "We have no choice. We have to go on with my plan."

They went back to the work tent together. Rafael and Maria had gone. After several faulty tries that awakened some very indignant Mexicans, Rod was finally able to reach the sleepy pilot.

"You will meet us in five days, not four," he instructed. "Is that clear?"

"*Si*, señor. In five days. You have more work to do?"

"I've learned some things I want to check out, but I want no one to know about it. If anyone asks, you intend to pick us up in four days as scheduled, okay?"

"*Si. Si.*"

When he'd hung up, Cara was staring at him. "What are you planning to check out?"

"Don't worry about it. The less you know the better."

Her gaze narrowed. "Rod Craig, if this is something serious that affects WHS Engineering, not to mention my life, then you'd better spill it right now."

He grinned at her. "Or what?"

"Or I'll stay right here and let you go back to the dam site alone."

"You want to stay here with Jorge?" he inquired very, very softly. There was a coldness in his eyes that Cara had never seen before. It should have made her wary. Instead, it simply baffled her.

"Jorge? What does he have to do with this?"

"I saw the way he looked at you earlier. Nothing would please him more than to have you all to himself."

Cara bristled. "And what if that's true? It's none of your business."

With a swiftness that set off alarm bells inside her, he hauled her against him. Fire had replaced the chill in his eyes. "It is very much my business, princess, and you know it."

Before she could react, his lips, his touch claimed her with a savageness that robbed her of breath. His fingers tangled in her hair and held her head still for the demand of his kisses. The protest that had formed on her lips ended in a whimper of pleasure as her body yielded to his possessive touch. Her struggle stilled as he cupped her against the hard cradle of his thighs, his arousal hot and pulsing against her. Her blood raced, sending fire through her veins. Her legs shook as anticipation swept through her.

Rod responded to her trembling by sweeping her off the ground and carrying her through the camp. Cara buried her face against the hot flesh of his neck, her tongue daring to taste the saltiness, to savor the frantic pounding of his pulse. This was what she wanted, what she'd been waiting for, perhaps since the first moment she'd seen him.

"Where are we going?"

"Your tent."

"But Maria..." she began with a frustrated groan.

He chuckled and brushed a consoling kiss across her lips. "I'm sure she is well occupied with Rafael."

When they were inside the tent, he lowered her slowly to her feet, allowing her body to slide along his. Then he stood away from her, only his eyes searing her. With one finger he reached out and touched her breast, a caress so light it might never have been except for the agonizing pleasure it left behind. Cara gasped, her eyes wide. She waited for what seemed an eternity for him to reach out to her again.

This time he bent and claimed her throbbing nipple with his mouth, moistening her shirt and creating a tormenting friction that sent waves of ecstasy rippling through her to center between her legs. When both nipples were hard, he lifted her top and ran a finger from breast to waist. His eyes locked with hers, he unsnapped the waistband of her pants, then lowered the zipper so slowly that Cara thought she would scream from the agony of waiting. When he kissed her bare belly, the shock ripped through her. She dug her nails into his shoulders as her body arched into the kiss.

"Rod, please."

"Not yet, princess. Not yet." He reached for the moist core at her center, caressing with a relentless, devilish expertise that left her breathing ragged and her body limp and slick with perspiration. When the waves of ecstasy subsided, she regarded him with confusion.

"Why?"

"Because it's been a very long time for me, princess, and I wanted to be sure this experience was everything it should be for you. Once I touch you, once I feel you around me, I might not be able to control myself long enough to give you the satisfaction you deserve."

The implications of his words registered dimly in the back of her mind, and she promised herself she would think about them later. But for now she wanted to know the sensation of being filled by him, of becoming part of his strength, of riding with him to the ends of the universe and back. It was her turn to give unselfishly to him.

She cast aside the rest of her clothes, then reached for his. When her fingers grazed his chest, she heard his sharp intake of breath, felt the rise of heat in his flesh. She wanted to explore, to know every inch of his magnificent body, but Rod's impatience took over.

"Sorry, princess," he apologized as he laid her gently on her cot, then braced himself over her. "I have to have you now. I've wanted you for so long." He entered her with one swift, sure thrust.

"For so long," he murmured against her cheek as his strokes filled her. Her hips rose to meet each one, the rhythm wild, uncontrolled. With one final surge, he exploded inside her, lifting her to yet another peak from which she felt sure she could see the entire world in all its splendor.

They collapsed together, cramped on the uncomfortable cot, but unaware of anything but their own feeling of well-being. Fear, anger, disappointment and doubts had fled for a time, replaced by joy and hope.

"Are you okay?" he murmured at last.

"Okay?" she murmured incredulously. Her leg still draped intimately across his, her fingers resting where she could feel the steady rhythm of his heart, she said honestly, "I never expected to experience anything like this."

The apparent awe in her voice seemed to amuse him. He lifted her hand and kissed each one of her fingers. "Not every jungle venture has this benefit, so I wouldn't be too quick to give up your seat in the boardroom, if I were you."

"I was referring to my entire lifetime. I thought these feelings only happened in books. Maybe in dreams."

"I think I can promise that you're not dreaming."

"Care to prove it?"

"Not on this cot, princess. The whole time I was making love to you, I had one eye on you and the other on the floor, where I was certain we were headed."

"And here I thought I had your undivided attention."

Rod rolled over and settled her on top of him. "Maybe not undivided, but you certainly had all the best parts."

"What arrogance!"

"Is it really? Didn't I live up to all the gossip?"

"Don't fish for compliments." Cara suddenly recalled his earlier comment. "Speaking of gossip, though, you said something when we came in here about it having been a very long time for you."

"So?"

"That doesn't quite fit with the image. I was under the impression you had a woman waiting for you in every major city."

"I guess I don't get to major cities all that often."

"I'm serious. Why did you let me believe that?"

"I thought it might get you to keep your distance."

"Is there the tiniest suggestion in that statement that I'm the one who seduced you?" she inquired indignantly. She sat up, straddling his middle.

"Not for a minute," Rod said, laughing at the menacing glare she'd feigned. "From the minute you stalked into the river the day you arrived, I knew I was in trouble. I figured my control was questionable, at best. I thought perhaps yours would be even better if you persisted in thinking I was an unrepentant rake."

She leaned down and kissed him lightly. "I must say I'm rather relieved. I discovered with Maria that I'm not as immune to jealousy as I would have liked.

It would have been a nasty business if I'd started roaming the world shooting down the competition.''

She caught the pleased gleam in his eyes before he could hide it. ''You would have liked that, wouldn't you?'' she said in astonishment. He looked ever-so-slightly guilty.

''It would have been flattering,'' he admitted.

''But costly. The legal fees would have been horrendous.''

''Then I guess it's a good thing we clarified things now.''

Her expression sobered with disgusting swiftness. ''Have we, though?''

''Have we what?''

''Clarified things. It seems to me we might have only muddled them.''

Rod sighed and drew her down until she was tight against him again. His hands stoked her back and hips with devastating effect. ''Ah, Cara, you still want simple answers, don't you?''

''Is that so wrong?'' she asked, her voice breathless.

''No. I'm just not so sure it's possible.''

He kissed her then, with a slowness that inflamed her senses. But when she would have drawn out the moment until rapture claimed them again, he lifted her up and got to his feet.

''I think it's time we both get some sleep. We have a long hike ahead of us. I want to get back to the dam site in two days.''

Knowing he was right didn't make it any easier for her to watch him leave. Though she had never spent any more perfect hours, she was left with the disturbing sensation that tonight could have been an end just as easily as a beginning.

Chapter Nine

They rose at dawn, joined the others for a light meal, then prepared to leave the archaeological site. For Cara the departure couldn't come quickly enough. As they were packing up, Rafael attempted a subtle cross-examination.

"So, señorita, the visit has been useful to you?"

Thinking of the conversation she'd overheard the previous night, Cara found it difficult to be courteous. Swallowing a quick, angry retort, she merely said, "Yes. Very informative."

The hint of sarcasm went unnoticed by everyone but Rod. He shot her a warning look as Rafael's gaze turned speculative. Fortunately Rod was able to salvage the tense moment. Nothing in his own behavior hinted at any of the suspicions they had. When Rafael questioned him, he gave an impressively calm, noncommittal reply.

"As you know, there are many factors to be considered and the decision is not just in my hands or in Cara's. The final decision will be made in Mexico City."

Rafael pressed. "But you will make a recommendation?"

"Our report is not yet final."

With a disappointed shrug, Rafael backed down.

Cara watched Maria's face during the exchange. Maria seemed troubled, though whether by Rafael's persistence or by Rod's responses it was difficult to tell. Jorge, on the other hand, appeared oddly amused by his boss's failure to get a commitment from them. Cara wondered if there was more of a rivalry between the two men than she'd previously guessed. Until last night, she had liked both men and felt that despite their very different personalities, they made an effective team. Perhaps Jorge's intolerant attitude toward Maria's idealism extended to Rafael as well.

Though Cara's farewells were cool, Rod's were astonishingly effusive—at least to Rafael, Maria and the other workers. In fact, he reserved his only scowl for Jorge, who admittedly prolonged his gallant kiss of Cara's hand a moment or two longer than was necessary. Then, oblivious to Rod's mounting irritation, he insisted on accompanying them for the first mile or so of the hike.

Once Jorge departed and they were alone, Rod set an even more punishing pace than he had on the long trek to the site. As if to emphasize his displeasure, he ignored her, his shoulders stiff, his expression disapproving.

Uncertain about what exactly had infuriated him, Cara tried every tactic she could think of to improve his mood. She chatted, she teased, she even tried flattery. She told him—quite truthfully, actually—how masterfully she thought he'd handled Rafael, when she'd been about to reveal too much. Every comment was met with stony silence.

"Don't tell me you're jealous," she taunted finally, practically running to keep up with him. Despite her excellent condition, she was already panting from the stifling heat. If she didn't get through to him soon, she was going to melt into a little puddle.

"Nope."

"Then why are you acting like this?"

"Like what?"

"Don't be obtuse, too. You know perfectly well you're acting like a predatory beast whose mate has been compromised."

"If you want to discuss Jorge Melendez, be my guest," he said, no longer pretending to miss her point. "I don't want to waste my breath. We have a long way to go."

And that, it appeared, was that. He clamped his mouth shut and marched on, leaving Cara to struggle along as best she could. She spent the time muttering about irrational men and trying to catch her breath.

By midmorning the sun was blistering. Not even the canopy of trees could protect them from its sweltering heat. When they'd been walking for three hours or more, Cara could no longer hide her exhaustion.

"Rod, we have to stop for a few minutes."

"We'll break for lunch in another hour or so. We should be back at the river by then."

"Dammit, I need a break now. Can't you at least stand still long enough for me to catch my breath and take a drink of water?"

He stopped, but his entire stance radiated his impatience. Cara opened her canteen and drank greedily. Before she realized Rod had moved, he was jerking the canteen from her hand.

"Slow down," he said gruffly. "You'll make yourself sick."

"I'm surprised you care."

He sighed heavily and ran his fingers through his damp hair, leaving it in a tangle of dark waves. His eyes met hers, then looked away. "Of course I care."

"Then do you suppose you could try and explain why you've been in such a foul humor? Was it Jorge?"

He shrugged. "Jorge. Rafael. Maria. Take your pick."

"You're angry at them, so you're taking it out on me?"

"You're here." He grinned ruefully. "Not a very good reason, is it?"

"Not especially, but probably to be expected."

"Oh, and why is that, Freud?"

"You're used to growling around like a wounded bear all alone. You've been able to indulge your moods to your heart's content. Having me in your life is a new experience. You haven't modified your behavior yet."

That earned a booming howl. "Modified my behavior?"

She glowered at him. "You know what I mean. Two people who've been living alone have to get used to living together."

His eyes narrowed at once, turning dark and forbidding. "That's a mighty big leap you're taking from one night in a tent to living together."

Cara felt a slow burn of embarrassment creep up her neck. "Dammit, stop deliberately misunderstanding me. I'm not talking lifelong commitment here. For better or worse, you and I are living together for the moment. Got it?"

Instead of exhibiting relief, his expression turned even more grim. "For the moment?"

Cara's patience snapped. "Oh, for heaven's sake. Make up your mind. When you thought I meant forever, you couldn't put me straight fast enough. Now that I'm agreeing with you that this is temporary, you're growling again."

"It is rather confusing, isn't it?" he said quietly. Then without another word, he capped the canteen and set off.

*   *   *

Rod knew he was being insufferable. The week or
so since Cara had turned up in Mexico had been the
most confusing time of his life. Every instinct inside
him had shouted that he should resist her, for her sake
as well as his own. This life-style suited him. She obviously hated it. Big cities gave him claustrophobia.
She adored living in New York. She wanted a stay-at-
home husband. He had wanderlust. It would never
work. Everything about her drove him crazy. He
should have been immune to her, but the irritating,
captivating, contradictory woman had breached every
one of his considerable defenses.

His body ached for her from morning to night.
And he was absolutely terrified that sooner or later
this danger would explode beyond cat-and-mouse
games and that he wouldn't be able to protect her. If
he loved her and lost her, he wasn't at all sure he
could live with himself. So, he thought decisively, he
simply wouldn't love her. No problem. He wasn't
some simpering, lovesick teenager incapable of con-
trolling his own emotions.

Instead, he growled at her, ignored her and
generally behaved like an absolute jerk, when what he
wanted to do was hold her and make love to her until
their bodies were slick with sweat and their hearts
were thundering in tandem as they had been the previous night. The tantalizing thought sent a rush of
blood straight to his loins. He almost stumbled as the
full force of his desire rocked him. So much for noble intentions and self-control.

"Damn," he muttered under his breath.

"What's wrong?" she asked.

"Nothing."

She nodded and retreated, but not before he'd seen the flash of hurt shadow her eyes. He swore softly and stopped so suddenly she slammed into him. He turned and caught her as she staggered from the impact.

"Are you okay?"

Breathless, she gazed up at him and he saw the tears shimmering in her eyes. With a proud lift of her chin, she was trying desperately to blink them away. One daring tear slid down her cheek. He brushed it away and felt the cold spot inside him begin to melt, along with his resolve.

"I'm sorry, princess."

"Ever since you and I met, there have been entirely too many apologies floating around," she said wearily. "Maybe we should think about why."

"Because I'm a heel."

"No, because we're both trying too hard to be something we're not." She took a deep breath and met his gaze evenly, her blue eyes luminous. He sensed she'd made a decision about something and that he wasn't going to like it. He suddenly felt as though the breath were being squeezed from his chest as he waited for her to finish.

"I think this is the wrong time and wrong place to even be thinking about a relationship. Maybe we're even the wrong people. For now, let's go back to being nothing more than two professionals with a job to do."

"And you can do that?" he asked dubiously but willing to grasp at any straw that might get them out of this jungle alive and with their emotions intact.

"Absolutely." Her voice shook only slightly when she said the word. He had to admire her courage. At the same time, he was not one bit sure he could do as she asked. His last resolution had lasted no more than sixty seconds.

"We'll give it a try," he said anyway.

Cara made an obvious effort to see that her decision worked out for the best. As she had earlier, she chattered away about everything from the macaws overhead to Donald Trump's skill as a businessman. Her comments were enthusiastic, perceptive, intelligent.

Rod didn't give a damn about any of it. In fact, he was so intent on watching the subtle sway of her hips, the spark of humor that lit her eyes that he missed the tree limb that had fallen and was hidden by brush. It hit him across his shin, sending him crashing forward. As he fell, a wrenching pain shot from his ankle all the way up his calf.

Cara was at his side at once, her expression filled with concern. "Are you hurt?"

"Only my pride," he said with a wry grimace.

She regarded him disbelievingly.

"Really. It's nothing serious. I just twisted my ankle. I'll be fine in a minute." Perspiration broke out across his brow. The sharp pain had diminished now to a steady, teeth-gnashing throb. He took a deep breath and stood up, unconsciously shifting all his weight to his left foot. A surprising wave of nausea washed over him. "Let's go."

Cara was watching his face intently. "Sit down," she ordered quietly.

"Come on, Cara. We don't have time for this."

"Fine. Go. You're white as a sheet. You'll probably make it about two feet before you fall flat on your face. I think I'll just sit here and watch." She sat down.

Irritation bubbled up inside him. He knew perfectly well she was right. He also knew they didn't have time to waste. Tentatively he took a step on his right foot. An agonizing pain soared through him. He clenched his fists, sucked in his breath and took another step on his good foot. Then another. The bad ankle gave way and he felt himself pitching forward. Cara was there to break his fall. She helped him to the very limb that had brought about the accident. He sank down and leaned his back against it, his whole body quivering from the strain. He closed his eyes.

"Let me see it," Cara said.

"It's sprained, okay? There's no need for you to examine it."

"Oh, will you just shut up and hold your leg still?" She put a restraining hand on his calf. His ankle hurt so badly, he couldn't even enjoy her touch. She untied his boot and gently removed it, then pulled off his sock. Rod didn't even want to look. He knew the ankle was already swollen. He didn't need Cara's cautious probing to make a diagnosis.

"It doesn't appear to be broken, thank God," she murmured.

"I told you it was sprained."

She reached for her backpack.

"What are you doing?"

"I have an elastic bandage in here. It may help." With brisk efficiency, she opened the package and wrapped his ankle, while he stared in astonishment.

"You can close your mouth now," she said finally, grinning at him. "Scottie insisted on thorough first-aid training, and Louise packs my supplies. I'm prepared for almost anything."

She propped his leg up on their backpacks. "Keep this elevated. I have some painkillers if you want them."

"I don't suppose you have a bottle of Scotch tucked in there instead," he inquired hopefully.

"Afraid not."

"Then skip it. We might as well have lunch. By the time we finish, I should be able to walk again."

"Forget it. You're not putting any weight on that ankle today."

"Cara, we don't have time for me to sit around babying this ankle. We have to get back to camp, dismantle everything and meet that plane."

"Fine. I'll go. You can wait here, and when the pilot shows up, we'll come back for you."

"Are you out of your mind? I'm not letting you take off through this jungle alone. You'll be lost in ten minutes." He refused to voice his primary fear, that alone she would be a tempting target.

Her only response to his concern was to pluck a compass from her pack and hold it out in front of him. "Just point me in the right direction."

"No."

"Stop being such a stubborn, macho jerk."

"When you stop being so bullheaded and irresponsible."

Glare met glare. Neither of them backed down, but it was Cara who spoke next.

"It is not irresponsible to want to see that this job gets done. Just this once can't you rely on me for a change?"

He noted that she didn't deny being bullheaded. "You won't be able to do it if you're lost."

"I'm not going to get lost," she insisted, waving the compass under his nose.

Rod grabbed his own backpack and began yanking out the tins of food. He opened a can of tuna fish and handed it to Cara. "Eat. We'll discuss it after lunch."

"There's nothing to discuss."

"Eat." His voice rose ominously. Cara regarded him mutinously, but she took the tuna.

As they ate, Rod tried frantically to think of an alternative course of action. He didn't think they should be separated, not with just one gun for protection. He was also forced to admit that there was no way he could walk any distance on his ankle at least for another twenty-four hours, if then. Despite his considerable imagination and experience, he couldn't think of anything better than Cara's plan.

He sighed heavily. "We'll make a deal."

Her eyes lit at once with interest. "What?"

"If my ankle's no better in the morning, you can go on."

"But we'll lose half a day."

"In the morning, Cara."

She directed a piercing look straight into his eyes, but when his determination didn't falter, she nodded.

"Now would you come here?" he suggested.

"What for?"

He grinned at her immediately suspicious demeanor. "Scared?"

"Of course not."

"Well, then?"

"We made an agreement," she accused. "This is going to be a strictly professional relationship."

"Did I say a single thing to suggest I had anything else in mind?" he said innocently.

"I don't trust you."

He shook his head sorrowfully. "Not a good basis for a *professional relationship*, princess."

She frowned at the deliberate taunt and stepped to his side. "Yes?"

"Closer."

With obvious reluctance, she stooped down. Rod felt only a fleeting instant of guilt as he captured her head and drew her closer still for a long, satisfying kiss. Her struggle was astonishingly halfhearted, her capitulation complete. But when he released her, she instantly began sputtering with indignation.

"You promised!"

He grinned. "Too late to protest, princess. You kissed me back. Besides, the temptation was entirely too great. I couldn't possibly resist, especially in my weakened condition." He tried to sound pitiful. She didn't appear to buy it.

"Your weakened condition!" She hooted. "Give me a break. Your hormones would probably be active in the midst of an earthquake. A piddly little ankle injury isn't going to keep you in check."

He laughed. "If you know that, then it wasn't very clever of you to get so close, was it?"

"Rod Craig, you are the most maddening man I have ever known in my life." Despite her tone, he could have sworn her lips were twitching with laughter.

"I don't doubt it. That's precisely why you can't resist me."

The hint of laughter died. Her eyebrows rose at least a half inch. "Can't resist you?" she growled. "I'll show you how irresistible you are."

She whirled around and stomped off, Rod's laughter following her. He knew she wouldn't stay away long. She'd forgotten her compass and her water and her backpack. No matter how infuriated she was with him, she wouldn't be foolish enough to leave without those.

When two hours had passed, though, and she still hadn't returned, he began to get nervous. He dragged the last of his cigarettes out of his pocket and lit it. His fingers trembled ever so slightly.

Damn! Why had he insisted on baiting her? Probably because he enjoyed seeing the way her blue eyes sparkled with indignation, the way her chin jutted out defiantly in her refusal to back down. Her spirited responses entranced him. But this time...this time what if they'd gotten her in trouble? She could be lost, or hurt, or someone could be stalking her, waiting to attack. The images were driving him crazy.

He dragged himself to a long, sturdy branch and began chopping at it with his machete. It was an awkward process from a sitting position. When it finally came free, he tested it to see if it would support his weight. He stood slowly and balanced himself against the makeshift cane. It wasn't ideal, but it would do.

With halting, painful steps he began his search. His heart pounded dully in his chest. What ifs tormented his thoughts. He tried to remind himself that Cara was the most amazingly resourceful woman he'd ever met. She was a survivor. No matter what had happened, she would have kept a cool, rational head. He reminded himself of all that over and over again.

It didn't help. He kept seeing her frightened and alone, and all because of him and his deliberately provocative goading.

He struggled on, easily noting the route she'd taken because of the trampled brush. She couldn't be lost. Surely even an amateur like Cara could have found her way simply by backtracking over the same trail. So where the hell was she? A shiver of dread ran down his spine.

When he first heard the rustling of leaves, he thought it was only a monkey swinging overhead. Even so, he paused where he was and waited, his senses alert. The noise increased, moving closer. Then Cara burst through the undergrowth, her face flushed, her hat askew. A relief as profound as anything he'd ever experienced rushed through him. He held out his one free arm and without a moment's hesitation she ran into his embrace. Either she'd forgiven him or she was terrified.

"Oh, Rod." The words came out in breathless gasps. His pulse raced.

"What is it?" he demanded at once, his heart lodged in his throat. "Are you all right? Is someone after you? Dammit, Cara, if anyone's hurt you, I'll kill them. I swear I will."

He felt her narrow shoulders began to shake, and her whole fragile body trembled in his arms. His imagination ran wild. Guilt rampaged through him. He tightened his embrace and tried to soothe her. His comforting caresses only seemed to set off more violent trembling.

"Oh, princess, I'm sorry. I shouldn't have teased you. I would have died myself rather than let anything happen to you. Please, it's going to be okay. You're with me now, and I promise I won't let anything hurt you ever again."

"Keep going."

His heartbeat slowed at the softly spoken words. "Keep going?" he repeated suspiciously. Her held her away from him and got his first good look at her expression. She was laughing, howling, in fact. Big tears were rolling from radiant eyes filled with mirth.

"You're okay, aren't you?" he said cautiously, just in case it was only a hysterical reaction and she really had been hurt.

"Disappointed?"

He dropped his hand to his side and scowled at her accusingly. "Of course, I'm not disappointed, though I am very tempted to wring your neck. You scared the hell out me."

"Serves you right."

He thought about her charge. "Probably," he admitted finally. "Now that you've gotten even, would you mind explaining what you were so upset about when you came tearing back here?"

"I wasn't upset. I was excited." He could read her enthusiasm in her eyes and in that eager-to-get-going stance. "Wait until you see what I found."

"What?"

"I'm not going to tell you. You have to see it for yourself. Do you think you can walk a little way? It's not far."

He took her hand. "To see what put that look in your eyes, I'll manage."

Fortunately, they didn't need to travel more than a half a mile or so. Suddenly they emerged into an area that had been partially cleared and he saw at once what had left her breathless. It was an archaeological site, one he knew from his maps and from talking with Rafael had never been reported. Even without

Rafael's expertise, he recognized this as a stunning find, one that should have drawn major attention.

At least three pyramids had been somewhat exposed, along with a number of smaller structures. None were as towering as the Temple of the Inscriptions at Palenque, but the detailed panels of carvings were every bit as spectacular and the scope rivaled what he'd read of the Mayan city of El Mirador now being excavated in Guatemala.

"Isn't it incredible?" Cara enthused. "I couldn't believe it. I've been climbing over the site for the past two hours. Why didn't Rafael mention this place?"

Rod shook his head. "I don't know. Maybe he doesn't know about it."

"How can that be? Surely the archaeologists stay on top of what sites are being worked."

"I would think so. I think there's some sort of procedure for registering them with the National Institute of Anthropology and History in Mexico City."

Her expression sobered at once. "Something's bothering you, isn't it?"

"You've already put your finger on it. A site like this," he said slowly. "Why wouldn't Rafael know about it?"

He approached the closest pyramid and ran his fingers across the surface of the stone. It was gray and pockmarked. The ravages of time. And yet . . .

He leaned down for a closer look, and his lips tightened. There were scars here that hadn't been made by nature. Pieces of a puzzle suddenly appeared and fell into place.

"What is it?" Cara asked.

"I think I've just figured out why someone's out to get us."

"I don't understand. What do these pyramids have to do with us?"

"Don't you see? They don't give a hoot about the long-range ecological disadvantages of the dam or even the principle of destroying the Mayan ruins. This—" he waved his arm in an all-encompassing gesture "—this is what they were worried about. They didn't want an outsider in the area even making a study. They were afraid we'd stumble across this site."

"So what? I would have thought they'd use this as another argument against the dam."

"They would if it had ever been reported, if they truly cared about saving the ruins."

"Rod, will you get to the point!"

"Can't you tell, Cara? Feel this," he said. He took her hand and rubbed it over the face of the stone. "The carvings haven't just worn away or broken away. Someone stumbled across this and decided there was more to be gained by keeping it a secret. They've been systematically looting it for who knows how long. They've probably been slipping across the border into Guatemala with the relics for months now."

Her eyes widened. "Thieves?"

"Exactly. Greed, not ideals, is behind all the attacks."

"What are we going to do about it?"

"That, princess, is the $64,000 question. My guess is we'd better get back to Mexico City and see someone at the Museum of Anthropology."

"Couldn't we tell Rafael and Maria?"

"You heard them last night. Do you think we dare trust them?"

"No. I guess you're right. I just keep thinking how thrilled they would be."

"You're assuming this place would be a surprise to them," he said with an edge of bitterness. Only twenty-four hours ago, he, too, would have wanted to share this with his old friend Maria. Now, all he had were doubts.

Cara sighed and took his hand in a gesture of comfort. "I hate this."

"Me, too, princess." He pulled her into his arms and held her. "Me, too."

They decided to set up camp overnight at the peak of one of the pyramids, which had been almost completely excavated. The stars seemed to be at their fingertips, diamonds scattered across black velvet. A carpet of vibrant green, lit by moonlight, lay spread out below. Despite her vow to maintain a professional distance between them, Cara gave a resigned shrug and settled down for the night in Rod's embrace. He didn't have the power to resist. He just drew her close and fought the desire to take much more that what she was offering.

When he awoke, the first pale light of morning was breaking through the trees. He rolled over and reached for Cara. She was gone.

She's probably off exploring again, he told himself as he stretched and tested his ankle. It seemed much better. He still couldn't put his full weight on it, but with the assistance of the cane, he could probably make it. The need to get back was made even more urgent by this latest discovery.

He checked out their limited food supply and prepared a breakfast of peanut butter and stale crackers. Disgusting, but reasonably nourishing. They'd used the last of their coffee the night before, but there were two cartons of juice left.

"Cara!" His shout echoed back to him, but there was no answering call. A prickling sensation ran along the back of his neck. "Cara!"

He limped awkwardly down the steep steps to the base of the pyramid, then, hobbling as fast as he could, he circled the site. With each step, his panic increased.

She was nowhere to be found. Had she left him and started back on her own? Spurred on by desperation, he made the agonizing climb to the top of the pyramid to check. Everything was right where it had been the night before—the compass, her backpack, her water. His heart sank.

A dozen scenarios, each more horrifying than the one before, played through his mind. This time the sick feeling in the pit of his stomach, the painful constriction in his chest, told him there was no mistake. This time Cara truly had vanished.

Chapter Ten

Cara came to slowly, her body aching, her lungs fighting for more of the stale, damp air. A strip of cloth that smelled sharply of oil and sweat had been used to gag her. Her stomach rolled over at the repugnant stench. Another rag had been tied around her head as a blindfold. Her arms had been bound behind her, her legs secured at the ankles. From the itchy, coarse feel of it against her bare arms, she was lying on a pile of burlap.

She felt like a trussed-up chicken. A stupid trussed-up chicken, at that. She kicked both feet in an awkward, useless gesture of protest.

She still couldn't figure out how those men had taken her by surprise. She'd slipped out of Rod's arms before dawn for a necessary trip into the brush. The hot, humid air had been still. No raucous birdcalls had split the silence. With the pyramids still awash with silvery shafts of moonlight, it had seemed incredibly peaceful, with just an edge of tantalizing mystery in the atmosphere. She had felt exuberant and content as she had contemplated watching the spectacle of a glorious sunrise from the pyramid.

Despite the overall feeling of serenity, she thought she'd been alert to every sound. She hadn't heard a single leaf rustle. One minute she had been straightening her clothes and the next she'd felt an arm around her neck cutting off the air. There had been no time to fight back, no time even to scream for help. She had heard a rapid, angry exchange of Spanish before the world faded into darkness.

Uncertain whether she was even alone now, she forced herself to remain perfectly still. She listened, but heard nothing. She had to think. She had to wait and rely on her senses to give her some clue that would explain where she was and who was holding her. She hadn't a doubt in the world, though, that her kidnapping was tied directly to the archaeological discovery she and Rod had made the day before and to all the other threatening incidents.

But in each of the previous situations, Rod had been there to lean on. Now, with his injured ankle, she couldn't count on him to charge through the jungle and rescue her. She was going to need all her wits about her to accomplish her escape. The prospect was daunting, but not impossible. She'd been independent far too long to panic over having to rely on her

own ingenuity now. She drew on every ounce of inner strength she'd inherited from Scottie. Combined
with some healthy outrage, a few well-learned self-
defense lessons and a survivor's passion for life, it
would get her out of this jam and back into Rod's
arms.

That optimistic note cheered her considerably.
Unfortunately, the mood didn't last. It was dashed by
the eruption of another argument. The tone and
voices sounded vaguely familiar. She was sure they
belonged to the men who'd taken her captive. Though
the sound was muffled, possibly by no more than the
canvas of a tent, she could hear most of the words
distinctly. They were again speaking in Spanish,
though, and it took several minutes for her still-
groggy mind to begin adapting. When the translation finally began to sink in, she wasn't one bit happy
about the gist of the heated conversation.

"No, no, Tomas," one of the men pleaded urgently. "You heard what he said. We are not to touch
her. He does not wish to infuriate the gringo, only to
frighten him. She is to be returned to him unharmed,
when he has met our demands." His voice was a
scared whine.

"Don't be such an old woman," the other one retorted. "For what I have in mind, there would be no
scars. She is very beautiful. Skin so pale and soft
would look good against this dark flesh of mine, is
that not true?" Now his voice took on a belligerent
note. "We work hard. We take all the risks. Why

should we not have our fun? Why should he always tell us what to do?"

"He is the *jefe!*"

Jefe? What the devil was jefe? she wondered. *Leader? Boss? Godfather in some sort of South of the Border Mafia?*

"It does not make him God," the one called Tomas said recklessly. She wondered if the bravado would have held up in the *jefe*'s presence. "Without us, he is nothing. Yet he gets all the money. The señorita would make up for some of the difference."

The words he used next were beyond Cara's vocabulary, but the coarse laughter, which even the other man joined in, was not beyond her understanding. Disgust and the first real chill of fear washed through her. Just what she needed, a couple of lusty, amoral hombres who wanted to get even with their boss. The very thought made her skin crawl.

A soft whoosh of air told her that someone had entered the tent. With any luck it would be Tomas's spineless companion. He seemed like the type who might be cajoled into helping her.

"So, señorita," a throaty voice purred in English. Her heart sank as she recognized it. Tomas. A rough finger caressed her cheek. Cara concentrated very hard on an image of Rod to keep from gagging. "You are awake?"

He removed her blindfold. Determinedly, she kept her eyes closed, feigning unconsciousness. Apparently she didn't do such a good job of it, because without warning, he grabbed a handful of hair and brutally jerked her head up. He yanked the gag from her mouth. She could feel his eyes burning into her.

"Answer me," he demanded with another painful yank of hair.

There was no point in any further pretense of sleep. She opened her eyes and glowered at him. She refused to acknowledge the pain shooting across her scalp. A bully like this one probably thrived on whimpers of agony.

"Yes?" she said politely, making a conscious decision to speak in English.

His gap-toothed grin reminded her of Carlos, but though her pilot had been slightly lecherous, there had been none of this man's malevolence about him.

"Better," he said approvingly. "You and me, we understand each other, *si*?"

"Who are you?"

"I wish to be your friend, señorita." The disgusting purr was back in his voice.

Cara saw no advantage in pursuing that particular discussion. "Where have you brought me?"

He waved aside the question. "You do not know the place."

If she could only see her watch, though, she bet she could figure out how far they were from where she'd been captured. Surely this camp wouldn't be far from the ruin, if these men were among the thieves.

"Could you untie my hands, please?" She injected an entirely unfamiliar note of humble supplication into her voice.

He shook his head adamantly.

"Please. The rope is cutting into my wrists. Perhaps you could just loosen it."

His eyes narrowed suspiciously. "You think I am loco, señorita?"

"No, of course not. I am sure you wish to take very good care of me." She tried to give her words a suitable, if revolting, double meaning, but apparently the subtlety was beyond him.

"I bring you food," he said and left the tent.

Once he was gone, Cara looked around. She'd been right about the burlap. To her surprise, though, it was marked with the familiar insignia of an American grain company. Was that pure chance or was the grain exporter somehow involved in the smuggling operation?

Before she could think through the possibilities, Tomas returned with a tin plate of corn tortillas and beans. Once again she appealed to him to untie her hands, this time so she could eat.

"I feed you," he said with a certain amount of eagerness. Keeping her helpless obviously appealed to his baser macho instincts.

He sat down next to her then, deliberately placing his body close to hers. He scooped some beans into the middle of one of the tortillas, rolled it and held it out to her. Despite imagining all sorts of dire intestinal consequences, Cara took a tentative bite. It was actually quite tasty, she decided, then blanched when she saw Tomas take the next bite of the same tortilla. Even though she knew she would regret it later, she declined any more of the food. She lay down.

"Is not good enough for you?" he inquired with a sneer. "You eat the steak and drink only the best wine, señorita? Here such food is for men, not skinny gringas. You will eat our simple food when you get hungry enough."

Cara didn't doubt he was right. She just hoped she wouldn't have to go on sharing it with him. He ate what she had left with enthusiasm, drinking a beer to wash it down. Watching him tip the bottle up until the foaming liquid was dribbling down his chin, Cara got her first idea. She had to encourage him to get drunk. And then? Well, she would think of that when the time came.

"Do you suppose I could have a beer?" she asked.

"Why not?" he said expansively. "After a beer or two, who knows?" He leered at her. It made her blood run cold. Still, she kept smiling.

Tomas left the tent, returning about five minutes later with two beers in hand.

"We have a little party, señorita. Okay?"

She beamed at him. "Okay."

She even kept from recoiling in disgust when he rubbed his hand deliberately across her breasts. Inside, though, she felt dirty, abused. If she ever got away from here, she would spend the rest of her life washing away his filthy touch. He was just reaching for her again when his name was bellowed outside, followed by a spate of furious Spanish too rapid for her to follow. His hand suddenly shook and he turned pale, but the glint of fury in his eyes was frightening.

So, she thought. That must be the hated *jefe*.

Tomas reluctantly got to his feet and left her. It was only after he had gone that the trembling set in. Frantically she tried to recall the pleasure of Rod's caress, the way he had made her blood sizzle through her veins, the sweet throbbing he had set off inside her. She needed those memories to banish the horror of Tomas's rough, grasping hands on her body.

The day went on, hour after empty hour. It was the whining Mexican who brought her dinner. She had thought he would be easier prey for her wiles, but he was so scared of his own shadow, he barely even looked at her. He said nothing, and she wondered if he even spoke English. She didn't dare speak to him in Spanish. As long as they thought she didn't understand the language, they might be more likely to reveal information she needed to escape. The guard left as soon as she had eaten.

So, she decided reluctantly, as much as he frightened her, Tomas was her hope. Eventually, his massive ego and lechery could be turned to her advantage. During the next twenty-four hours, a plan began to form in her mind. It was a risky, daring plan. If it failed, she wasn't at all sure she could live with the consequences.

She had no alternative.

Rod thought he was losing his mind. Cara had been gone for nearly two days. Limping painfully, he had searched the immediate area, returning frequently to the archaeological site. He was convinced that this latest act of terrorism was tied to the smuggling they'd discovered. Sooner or later, whoever was responsible for Cara's disappearance would turn up at the site to resume the looting.

Late on the second day, he returned to the site and found a crudely scrawled note.

"You want gringa alive, you leave Mexico. No return. Ever. No dam. We let woman go free, when you gone."

From the awkward, ungrammatical sentence structure, Rod surmised the sender was relatively uneducated, at least in the English language. That left out Rafael and Maria, unless they had chosen to disguise themselves by appearing ignorant. For the life of him, he still couldn't imagine this as their style of protest. Rafael he didn't know well, but Maria he had known for years. She was as straightforward and direct a woman as he'd ever met. She would also know that there was no way in hell he'd ever leave Mexico without Cara. Kidnapping her would only make him more determined to unearth whatever scheme her captors were engaged in.

Ignoring the note's threat and knowing that he couldn't trust Cara's captors to honor their promise, on the third day he widened his search area. It was nearly noon when he sensed that someone was watching him. His hand hovering near the gun he had tucked in the waistband of his pants, he waited, peering into the shadows. Every muscle in his body was tensed. His nerves were stretched so taut that he was afraid the slightest movement would cause him to fire blindly into the brush. Just when he thought his control was at an end, four Lacandones appeared in front of him, their approach so silent it was as if they'd simply materialized. The fifth, the one who had objected so strenuously to the meeting with Cara, was missing.

Though they were the same men who had met with him and Cara, he still kept his hand near his gun as he greeted them. His proud gaze deliberately diverted from Rod's weapon, Juan Castillo stepped forward.

"You have trouble," he inquired, gesturing toward Rod's bandaged ankle.

"It is nothing," he said. "But, yes, there is trouble. Cara, the señorita, is missing. She has been kidnapped."

Rod's words seemed to puzzle him.

"Taken away," Rod explained.

The Lacandones's expression hardened at once. There was no sign of guilt, only concern. "She has been harmed?"

"I hope not, but I have no way of knowing. Do you know of other men in the jungle?"

He nodded at once and pointed in the direction of Rafael's camp.

"No. She would not have been taken there," he said with certainty. Even were Rafael and Maria involved, they would keep Cara far from any place he knew. There had to be more conspirators, another camp.

"Any other men?" he asked.

The leader shook his head, but one of the others stepped forward and murmured something. "My friend says there is another camp hidden not far from here, very close to the border with Guatemala.''

"Refugees?'' Hundreds had crossed Guatemalan borders into Mexico and set up camps, but he'd thought they were farther south.

"No. Not Guatemalans. He says these people are bad.''

"Why does he say that?''

"They are stealing.''

Rod felt his stomach tighten. "From the ruins?''

"*Si, si*. From the ruins.''

"Can he show me where this camp is located?''

"*Si*.''

At the leader's request, the man knelt down and drew a crude map in the mud. When he'd finished, the leader offered to come with Rod. "We would be five then. It is better than one man alone.''

Though he didn't want to endanger them, Rod knew he didn't dare turn down the assistance. With his ankle still weak, it might be crucial to Cara's safety to have someone with him who was more mobile than he was.

"*Gracias,*'' he said. "*Muchas gracias.*''

It was early evening when they reached the camp. At first it seemed there was no one around and Rod had to restrain the impulse to rush in immediately and search the tents for Cara. He knew his lack of patience could cost her life. It was vital that he watch and wait.

Eventually, a disreputable-looking Mexican emerged from one tent and began cooking over an open fire. When he'd finished, he hitched up his pants and puffed out his chest like a peacock about to embark on a mating ritual. Rod felt his stomach turn over. His blood roared in his ears as he watched the man take the plate to another tent and go inside.

"That's it," he murmured, his heart thundering. He could practically feel Cara's presence. "She has to be in there."

Again he had to resist the urge to go charging in after her, especially after seeing the man who was now in her tent. He knew with gut-wrenching certainty what was on the man's mind, and it made him physically ill. If that sleazy criminal so much as laid a finger on her, though, Rod knew he would kill him.

The Lacandones watched him closely. "She is here?" Juan Castillo asked.

"I'm sure of it."

"Then we get her," the leader said decisively, lifting his bow.

"Not yet," Rod said softly, reluctantly. There were still too many unknowns. "When darkness falls."

He hoped to God that wouldn't be too late.

Darkness couldn't fall soon enough for Cara. The days had begun to follow a pattern, and evening was the time she'd decided she had the best chance of succeeding with her plan. Tomas and her other guard, Luis, were beginning to get very nervous. Whatever their plan had been, it seemed to have gone awry.

Perhaps Rod was not cooperating with their demands. She had not heard the *jefe*'s voice for some
time now. However, only the fear of his sudden appearance had kept Tomas in check this long. His
crude innuendoes were becoming increasingly difficult to ignore.

Take advantage of them, she told herself. *Now.
Tonight, before it's too late.*

She took a deep breath and swallowed hard to hide
her fear. She managed a wavery smile. "Tomas, this
jefe, why is it that you don't like him?"

Fire burned in his eyes. He spit. "He is a fool. He
thinks he is better than the rest of us. You see how
good he is. This plan of his, *muy* loco. It is not working. No man would give up everything, just for a
woman."

"Give up what?" she asked, though she knew.
They'd asked for a commitment that there would be
no dam. Now even that probably would not be
enough. They would want guarantees that their
thievery would not be revealed.

"Does he want money?"

His gaze narrowed suspiciously. "No, señorita. No
money and no more talk."

Cara backed off immediately. She was certain she
had her answer anyway. Apparently it had never oc-
curred to these men that *she* might be the one who
would make the decision about the dam. They were
using her as a pawn with the man they thought held
the power.

"No more talk," she said agreeably. She forced a friendly smile. "How about a beer? I feel very thirsty tonight, Tomas. You would like to drink with me, perhaps?"

His gloomy expression brightened at once. "*Si. Si.* You and me, we have a good time tonight."

He left the tent and came back with several bottles of beer. He twisted off the caps, wiped the mouth of one on his filthy sleeve and offered it to her. She tried not to cringe.

"My hands," she reminded him. "I can't hold it. Maybe you could tie them in front. Then I could lift the bottle."

He considered the idea. "Why not?" he said expansively. He untied the rope that bound her, brought her hands around and repeated the elaborate knots. Cara accepted the beer, sipping it as he took a long, deep swallow of his own. Hopefully the man didn't have a high tolerance for alcohol, or this would be a very long night.

After he'd finished two more beers, Cara began to see signs of drunkenness.

"You know, Tomas," she said softly. "I think you were right. I think you and I do have something special between us. We are simpatico."

He beamed at her. "*Si. Si.* Simpatico." The words slurred ever so slightly.

Swallowing her revulsion, she reached out to touch his chest, making an elaborate show of the gesture's awkwardness, which resulted from her bound hands. She sighed dramatically.

"It is no use. I cannot touch as I would like, when I am tied up in this way."

A lecherous gleam lit his eyes. "I will untie you, señorita, and then I will show you what a real man is like. You would like that?"

"*Si,*" Cara said, barely choking the word past the lump in her throat.

Tomas drew his knife from the waistband of his pants and slashed it through the rope in a melodramatic display. He looked at the rope that bound her ankles consideringly, then slashed through that one as well. Then, after carefully replacing the sharp, gleaming, well-cared-for weapon in his leather holder, he grasped her hands and kissed them.

Don't pull away. Concentrate on the knife, Cara reminded herself in desperation. *If you can get the knife, you can get free.*

Tomas was groping for her breast. With clumsy, rough hands he tugged at her tank top, then yanked, splitting it down the front. Cara's eyes widened, but she swallowed a scream that threatened to erupt and shatter any chance of her escape plan succeeding. Tomas couldn't seem to tear his eyes away from her pale, creamy breasts, which were rising and falling with each anxious breath she took. They were barely shielded from his hungry gaze by her lacy bra.

Now. It has to be now, she thought and stepped closer, moving into his arms. His breath on her bare shoulder was hot, disgusting. She ignored it as she placed a hand on his back, moving it in what she hoped he would interpret as a caress, all the while wanting to run from this vile embrace.

Then her fingers found the handle of the knife. When she had it securely in her grasp, she raised her knee directly into Tomas's groin, drawing out the knife in the same instant. As he clutched himself in agony, she put the tip of the knife to the middle of his back.

"On the floor," she said, her voice controlled, exhibiting none of the panic she was feeling.

Uncertainty spread across his face. She nicked his flesh and he dropped to the floor at once. The rope that had bound her arms and feet was no longer useful after Tomas's slicing cut through the knots. She found the gag that had been used to keep her silent and wound it around his wrists. Improvising, she cut strips of the burlap and created an effective restraint for his legs.

Just as she was about to tie the first knot, he took advantage of her concentration and heaved his body over, knocking her off balance. Though she still held the knife, she was lying facedown, and his weight had her at a disadvantage.

"Now, señorita, we see who is stronger. You will pay for this."

The fury in his voice, the threat, sent bile to her throat. She struggled furiously beneath him. Rolling over and over, they slammed into the table that held the lantern and sent it crashing to the floor. Suddenly it was pitch black in the tent. Cara tried to get enough leverage to use the knife, not caring about the aim. When it struck flesh, there was a cry of outrage, and Tomas fought her even more viciously. Even injured and without the use of his hands, he was a formidable foe. Once more, he had her pinned facedown in the dirt, his knee in her back.

Then suddenly he was off her. As she gasped for breath, there was the sound of a brief struggle—flesh making impact with flesh, bones cracking and then a heavy thud. She sprang to her feet, taking a defensive stance, her eyes trying to accustom themselves to the shadows. Knife still in hand, she was prepared to go after Luis or the *jefe* or whoever had chosen to interfere. This was her only chance to escape. If she was going to die, at least they were going to know they'd been up against a fighter.

She saw Tomas's body slumped against the burlap, and what might be the figure of another man. Preparing herself to attack, she took one slow, cautious step before a voice cracked through the air, commanding, amused. It came not from the direction in which she was looking, but from behind her.

"You can put the knife down, princess."

Chapter Eleven

Just like that, the three-day ordeal was over. It took a moment for the realization to sink in. She was safe, Rod was here, Tomas was unconscious, and the horror was over—at least for now.

Cara released her pent-up breath, but the adrenaline continued to pump. Delayed panic whispered unexpectedly along her nerves and left her trembling. She sank down on the pile of burlap and peered up at Rod through the darkness. Even dirty, unshaven and tired, he had never looked more wonderful. Even with that familiar tone in his voice—half amused, half impatient—she'd never been happier to hear him.

"I think I'll just hang onto the knife a little longer, if you don't mind," she said in a shaky voice. "It makes me feel more secure."

The harsh line of his mouth softened slightly. "I could do that," Rod suggested quietly, dropping down beside her.

Then she got a really good look at his expression. It was far from the dispassionate one she'd expected.

Hazel eyes, darkened by a raw, passionate hunger, met hers. The gaze caressed and lingered as if an eternity would not be long enough to reassure him that she was uninjured. It was the look of a man who cared desperately, a man who had been afraid and wasn't quite sure how to deal with it. That open display of vulnerability, that need for reassurance robbed her of breath all over again.

The wrong-time-wrong-place refrain played through her head again. It was the only thing that kept her from flinging herself straight into his arms, where she knew she'd be welcomed and comforted and seduced. She struggled to bring a much-needed lightness into the breathless, sexually charged atmosphere.

With a glimmer of a smile, she pointed out, "It has come to my attention of late that you're not always around."

His own faint smile was rueful. "I'm here now."

"Exactly," she said with forced breeziness. "After I had everything under control."

He raised one eyebrow skeptically. "You were in control of that scene I walked in on?"

She paled at the memory of Tomas's body pressing down on hers. Even though the man's hands had been tied, it had been a too vivid hint of how things might have turned out.

"Well," she admitted, "there was just a moment there when I might not have been entirely in command of the situation."

Rod's jaw clenched and there was a dangerous glint in his eyes. "I'd say that's an understatement."

She hurried on, not allowing herself to dwell on the memory Rod's growled comment unleashed. "But his hands were tied. What could he have done, really?"

"I hate to think about it, princess." His voice was no more than an agonized whisper.

She didn't dare meet his eyes. She could not even bring herself to offer a reassuring touch. Her control over her emotions was too tenuous. If she allowed herself to relive the last few days, hysteria would set in. She would be useless to whatever plan Rod had in mind. She had to stay calm, controlled. She refused to crumble now. Her voice trembled as she forced a change in the disquieting conversation. "How did you find me?"

With the appearance of something akin to relief, Rod drew in a deep breath and accepted the diversion. He got to his feet and began pacing. He ran his fingers through his hair in an agitated gesture that had become endearingly familiar. Each time he neared Tomas's limp form, Cara had the feeling he was only barely resisting the urge to kick the man.

"The Lacandones helped," he said at last. "They're outside now, keeping an eye on things."

His expression turning grim, he became cold and businesslike. "Are there any more of these charming fellows around?" This time he did nudge Tomas with the toe of his hiking boot.

"I've heard several voices, but there's only one I've met, Luis. I haven't seen him since this morning—I guess it's yesterday morning, actually." Surely by now the entire night had passed. It seemed like an eternity. She shuddered again unconsciously.

"I don't think Luis is much of a threat," she went on finally, forcing her thoughts to focus on the present. "There's also some sort of boss they really seem to despise. As far as I could tell, he's the mastermind behind the smuggling. Neither Tomas nor Luis has the brains for it."

"I don't suppose you've had a chance to look around."

"No. I was unconscious when they brought me in, and I've been pretty much confined to my tent since then. Except for his sweet-talk, old Tomas here was pretty tight-lipped. I only know they were hoping you'd want me back badly enough to abandon the dam project."

"So they said."

Startled, she stared at him. "You've talked to them?"

"No. They left a ransom note of sorts at the pyramid. It made terrific bedtime reading." Control fled.

A low moan crossed his lips. "Oh, princess," he whispered raggedly.

She could no longer ignore his pain or her own need. She struggled to her feet. Holding her breath, this time in far sweeter agony, Cara anticipated his touch. Finally, finally, he tentatively put his hands on her arms as if she were fragile, precious. His eyes searched hers, a lifetime of emotion in the quiet scrutiny. "Are you really okay, princess?"

There was an astonishing quiver in his voice, as if he were struggling with some entirely unexpected, powerful emotion. Fear? Anger? Possibly—her heart lurched—possibly even love.

"I'm fine," she whispered, though her knees betrayed her by feeling like they'd turned to jelly once more. He caught her to his solid chest just before she could disgrace herself by falling. After all this bravado for his benefit, fainting would have been the ultimate humiliation. Still, she wasn't so set on courageousness that she couldn't enjoy the wonder of actually being back in Rod's strong, muscular arms. There had been moments, moments she had never once admitted to, when she'd been terrified that she would never feel his arms around her again.

Lifting her face to his, she saw once more that hunger that turned his eyes into fiery jewels. And then his lips were on hers. Tenderly. So tenderly, as if he feared she might yet break. Meant simply to restore warmth, his touch set off fire. His muscles were taut with the effort to restrain himself. It was Cara, finally, who deepened the kiss, whose tongue caressed and tasted and savored until Rod moaned and matched her intensity.

That kiss—passionate, lingering—restored strength, renewed her sanity. It banished terrible, frightening memories. It healed.

And, then, all too quickly, it had to end.

"We can't stay here," Rod murmured, still nibbling on her lower lip.

"I know." She kissed the corner of his mouth.

"I want you to go into the brush and wait with the Lacandones while I search the camp." His lips found a sensitive spot at the base of her throat.

Cara nipped his ear. "No way."

The playful tone vanished in an instant. Determination firmed lips that only a moment before had been softened by her caress. His jaw set stubbornly, but no more so than hers.

"Cara!" His voice rose ominously.

One blond brow rose in what Scottie would have recognized as a warning.

"I'm not going," she said softly, steel wrapped in velvet. "Just look at what happened the last time we got separated."

"I want you where you'll be safe."

"And what about you?"

He touched the gun at the waistband of his pants. "I have my own protection."

"And I have a knife now."

"It's not the same."

She gave him a disgusted scowl. "We're wasting time. I'm coming with you. I'm the one they kidnapped."

"Getting even is not on the agenda for the moment. I want to look around for a few answers, and then we're getting out of here the minute it's daybreak."

"I'm all for that, but I am not waiting in the jungle like some simpering, delicate flower while you snoop around satisfying your curiosity. We're partners in this."

This time his eyebrows rose skeptically. "Partners? Since when?"

"I was trying not to pull rank," she said demurely.

With that she turned and left the tent, leaving him staring after her. She counted her steps, guessing she had no more than ten before he'd catch up with her. Muttering expressively, Rod followed her. He grabbed her arm when she would have marched straight on to the next tent. She'd taken exactly nine steps.

"Slow down," he demanded. "If you insist on doing this, at least use your head. You don't know who might be lurking inside that tent. Old Luis could be in there after all."

"If he is, he's probably sleeping or passed out drunk."

"Or waiting with a shotgun."

Good point, she admitted, though not aloud. She did give him the satisfaction of going ahead of her. It wasn't that she was turning cowardly all of a sudden.

It was just the sensible thing to do. After all, Rod did have the gun.

To her disappointment—well, more or less disappointment—the tent was essentially empty. Rod lit a lantern and held it up to dispel the shadows. There were two cots, a carton of canned goods and a few cooking utensils. Still not speaking, he waved her outside.

Carrying the lantern, they approached the remaining tent with similar caution. Again, there were no sounds to indicate that anyone was inside, but he gave her the light to hold and motioned for her to wait. Almost as soon as he'd taken the first step inside, he came to an abrupt halt. She saw his hand move slowly. Her heart began to pound, but then she realized he wasn't reaching for his gun after all. He was holding out his hand for the lantern. She gave it to him. Once the soft glow erased the shadows inside, she heard his low whistle of astonishment.

"What is it?"

He stepped aside and held open the tent flap. "See for yourself."

She looked inside and gasped. Mayan relics filled the tent. Carvings, the most beautiful she'd ever seen, were stacked haphazardly. The amount of pottery was staggering. There were bowls and pitchers and other vessels, some plain, some decorated with hieroglyphics and simple figures. Some were broken or chipped, but even to her untrained eye it appeared that many of the pieces were museum quality. There were several limestone stelae, all carved, some decorated with the red paint that, according to her talks with Rafael and Jorge, held some religious significance.

"My God!" Cara breathed, excitement rushing through her. "It's incredible. This must be worth a fortune."

"I'm sure it is, especially on the black market," Rod said wryly. "Since law forbids the removal of these things from the country, private collectors with no scruples will pay dearly for them. I just wish I could figure out how they've been getting the things across the border. Not that the border isn't like a sieve down here, but I would think it would be difficult to move this much stuff without arousing suspicion."

"The burlap," Cara murmured to herself.

"What?"

"I was just thinking aloud." She continued to toy with the idea that was forming. "In the tent where they held me there were sacks of burlap. Didn't you notice it?"

"Princess, the only thing I noticed in that tent was that man attacking you."

"Well, the place was filled with burlap, all with the insignia of some American grain company. What better way to get something across the border without notice than by hiding it in a much-needed shipment of grain." She met his eyes. "What do you think?"

Rod swept her into his arms and planted a hard kiss on her lips. "You're a genius."

"Just observant," she said modestly. "Do you really think that's it?"

"I'd stake my career on it, which, by the way, I might have to do, if we don't get out of here and report in to Scottie soon. He must be frantic."

"What are you planning to do?"

"We'll get back to my campsite and clear everything up. It shouldn't take more than a few hours. Then we'll meet the pilot. We'll have him take us straight to Mexico City. I can't wait to turn this entire mess over to the authorities. Then I think WHS owes us both a long vacation."

Cara didn't allow herself to consider the implications of that remark. "What if the pilot's already left? We're late getting back."

"He won't leave. WHS is paying him very well to stick around until we turn up."

When they turned to leave the tent, they found the Lacandones waiting patiently outside. The first pale light of dawn was shimmering through the trees. In that subdued light, Juan Castillo studied Cara with serious eyes.

"You are well?"

"Si, gracias."

Apparently satisfied not so much by the answer as by what his eyes told him, he nodded slowly, then looked to Rod. "What will you do now?"

"We need to get back to my camp without anyone following us," Rod said. "Can you help us?"

"We will guard the man here and watch for others. One of my men will follow along the trail behind you, another will go in front. No one will approach unless you indicate that it is your wish."

Cara watched these two men, so newly acquainted, yet so obviously kindred spirits. Despite the vast differences in culture and life-style, they shared similar values and respect. Each, in some ways, thought the other was poor, yet neither made judgments.

"We will find some way to repay you, my friend," Rod promised. "Food, supplies, whatever you need."

"Our gods provide for us." There was no arrogance in the words, just supreme confidence in a way of life. Cara had never before witnessed such self-possession, such quiet command.

"Then we will send what the gods cannot provide," Rod said.

When they were on their way, Cara glanced at him. "What exactly do you think it's in your power to give them that their gods can't?"

"Some Mozart," he said with a grin. "Maybe a little Beethoven. I might even send along a tape of the Beatles. That should really confound them."

Cara laughed. "It might make more sense to send fishing rods," she said dryly.

"Ah, princess, you're entirely too practical sometimes."

"It comes in handy when you're trying to run a company."

Rod opened his mouth, but she held up a hand, "So help me, if you suggest I take time to stop and smell the roses, I will find a snake and tuck it into your sleeping bag."

For the first time since he'd found her, Rod's uninhibited laugh echoed through the jungle. "I don't
think I need to worry about that."

She regarded him suspiciously, just a little disappointed that he hadn't taken the admittedly idle threat
more seriously. "And why is that?"

He returned her stare with a look so innocent the
angels would have been fooled. "Scottie told me what
happened in Brazil."

Her eyes widened. Surely her father would not have
revealed that one time in her life when she had utterly and completely lost her cool. "What exactly did
Scottie tell you?"

"He said, and I quote, 'When she saw that snake
all curled up, the fool gal screamed so loud, you could
have heard her clear to Rio. I thought the whole damn
tent must have been on fire.'"

So much for her image as a woman who could
handle anything, a woman who could cope quite
nicely in any environment. For some reason, during
the past few days it had become increasingly important for her to prove that to Rod.

"Scottie talks entirely too much," she grumbled.

"Don't look so embarrassed, princess. He thought
it was cute. It made him feel needed."

"What about you? Do you suffer from the same
male malady?"

"Are you asking if I prefer my women to lean on
me?"

"More or less."

"I suppose every man likes to fall into the role of strong, male protector occasionally."

"Would you have preferred it if I'd swooned back there, so you could have ridden in on a white charger and saved the day?"

"I thought I had."

"Stop it. I'm serious."

He sighed. "Princess, I am very glad that you did not fall apart under pressure, that you had devised a scheme to escape. My ego can handle the fact that you don't have to rely on me to survive."

It was exactly what she'd wanted to hear. He had recognized her independence, her resourcefulness. But now that she'd heard the words, even though they'd been spoken with a certain amount of admiration, somehow they sounded hollow. Maybe he wasn't looking for a woman who could traipse to the ends of the earth with him after all. Hell, maybe she should have swooned. Her head hurt from trying to make sense of the situation. *Forget figuring out what Rod wants,* she told herself. She didn't even know what she wanted anymore. Aside from the obvious calamities, this trip was proving to be an emotional mine field.

They finished the hike in silence. When they reached the camp at midday, they made quick work of dismantling the remaining equipment. The two Lacandones helped them pack everything and carry it to the airstrip.

Whey they arrived, a small Cessna was waiting, just as Rod had predicted. There was no sign of the pilot, but the plane was unlocked. They loaded everything onto it.

"What do we do now?" Cara asked.

"We wait. I can't imagine the pilot's gone too far." He spoke to the Lacandones and, after a solemn farewell, they faded into the jungle.

"Why did you send them back?"

"There's no point in them hanging around here."

Just then Cara noticed a movement in the brush on the other side of the runway. "Did you see that?" She pointed. "Over there."

"Where?"

"In a straight line just past the nose of the plane. I saw something move."

"Wait here and I'll check it out."

He started forward, careful to keep the plane between him and the spot where she'd seen the movement. Cara was right on his heels. He shot a scowl over his shoulder, but didn't comment. Slowly a man emerged from the forest and Rod released a sigh of relief.

"No problem, princess. It's the pilot."

He had just opened his mouth to call out to the man, when Cara got a good look at him and gasped. "Luis?"

"No," Rod corrected, unaware of her sudden panic. "His name is Pedro Garcia."

"I'm telling you, it's Luis," she whispered.

Rod turned to stare at her. "Who the hell's Luis?"

"The other guy who was holding me."

He reached for his gun, but his instant of hesitation had cost him the advantage. Before he could get his fingers around his own weapon, a shotgun blast ripped past them. Rod grabbed the door of the plane and wrenched it open.

"Get in."

"I am not leaving you out here."

He grabbed her around the middle and tossed her through the door. She landed...hard. As he climbed in after her, Rod fired two shots that dug up dirt in front of the rapidly approaching Mexican. He slammed the door closed and jumped into the pilot's seat. He handed Cara the gun.

"If he tries to get in the door, shoot him."

The hand, which unexpectedly found itself in possession of a gun, trembled. "Shoot him?"

"If you have any problems with your conscience, just remember he's one of the men who kidnapped you."

That steeled her nerves instantly and she kept a steady aim at the door as Rod started the plane's twin engines. She heard Luis pounding uselessly on the door just before they took off down the short runway.

Then trees were rushing toward them. Panicked at the speed with which they seemed to be approaching certain death, Cara glanced over at Rod for reassurance. That was a mistake. He was holding the throttle with white-knuckled intensity. He also appeared to be murmuring a prayer.

"Oh, my God!" she whispered. She dropped the gun and held onto the edge of her seat. "Rod Craig, I did not survive that kidnapping and this awful jungle only to die in a plane crash with you! Do I make myself clear?"

"Perfectly, princess. I'm doing my best."

At the last possible instant, without so much as an inch of airstrip left, the plane lifted off, dipping slightly. The right wing clipped the top of a tree and the whole plane shuddered. It dipped left, then steadied.

Cara closed her eyes and swallowed hard. "I suppose this is not the very best time to be asking this question, but do you know how to fly this thing?"

"I got us up here, didn't I?"

"Barely."

He turned to look at her then. His brow was damp, his eyes tired, but there was the beginning of a grin tilting the corners of his mouth. "Don't look like that, princess. It wasn't bad for a man who's only had a couple of lessons."

Cara buried her face in her hands. Her heart thumped unsteadily. "Tell me, please, that one of those lessons included landing."

She did not like the evasive look in his eyes one little bit. He suddenly became extraordinarily interested in the control panel. That could be the sign of a pilot running through a standard checklist, or it could be the mark of a man who wasn't crazy about the question.

"Rod?"

"Would you rather hear the answer to that now or after we're on the ground?"

For the second time in five minutes, Cara saw her entire life flash before her eyes.

Chapter Twelve

When Cara could finally breathe again, she glanced at Rod. Despite the narrowness of the escape from Luis or Pedro or whoever the hell he was, despite coming within a hairbreadth of crashing, he actually seemed to be enjoying himself. Once a daredevil, she thought disgustedly. How had she ever forgotten, even for an instant, that the man was exactly like her father? Scottie would have been slapping his knee and chortling with glee right now, figuratively thumbing his nose at Luis, Tomas and their dreaded *jefe*. True, Rod's delight was more sedate. He merely looked smug.

"You don't plan to try to fly this thing all the way to Mexico City, do you?" Visions of colliding with a

jumbo jetliner danced in her head with sickening
clarity.

"No," he said and she actually thought she heard
a note of regret in his voice. "The authorities there
probably take a dim view of private planes being pi-
loted by men without licenses. They might actually
get it into their heads we were drug smugglers or
something."

"What an absolutely delightful thought," Cara
commented with deliberately exaggerated cheer. "So,
where are you planning to land? Palenque or Comitan?"

"I'd rather go to Tuxtla Gutierrez. It's a little farther, but we'd be able to get a flight there straight to
Mexico City."

Cara had no real objections to staying in the air
now that they were safely up here, especially if it
meant delaying even by a few minutes the moment
when they discovered the extent of Rod's skill at
landing. Tuxtla Gutierrez probably also had slightly
more experienced flight controllers who could talk
them down. She tried very hard not to recall the exact size of the plane she'd been on when she'd landed
there on the trip down. However, by comparison with
this tin can, it had definitely been in the jumbo range.

All she said to Rod was, "I suppose you know
where it is."

He immediately assumed an injured expression.
"Of course I know where it is. It's west," he said
confidently.

She was somewhat reassured.

"More or less," he amended.

Cara groaned. "Terrific."

"Okay. So, I'm not so sure how to get there. Dig around up here and see if there are any aviation maps. Then you might get on the radio and see if you can rouse the control tower."

"Me?"

"Hey, why not?"

"I'm just along for the ride."

"I don't want you to get bored."

"Believe me, I am never bored when I'm trying to survive." She shook her head in bemusement. "You're really enjoying this, aren't you?"

As the critical tone of her question registered, she watched his hand tighten on the throttle, saw him clench his teeth. The light in his eyes died. Somehow it all made her feel guilty.

"Do you want me to say no?" he asked in a flat voice.

She sighed deeply. "I don't want you to lie to me."

"Then, yes, I am enjoying it."

She struggled to understand what made him tick, as she'd never understood Scottie. "Is it the living on the edge? Do you like flirting with death?"

"No more than with a dangerous woman." He flashed a wicked grin at her.

She responded to the grin instinctively. Not many men had ever classified her as dangerous. Not the way Rod meant it. Cute, perky and feisty were about the best she'd ever done outside the corporate board-room. Inside, she knew what they thought of her, and dangerous was kindly by comparison. However, Rod's innuendo, though appreciated on some feminine level, was quite beside the point. She masked her momentary thrill of pleasure and snapped impatiently, "Rod!"

He sobered at once. He even managed to look contrite, which made her extraordinarily suspicious.

"Sorry," he said. "Of course not. I mean I don't enjoy being shot at any more than the next man. And it might have been nice to take you for a spin in this plane after I had a little more experience under my belt, but the truth is I like knowing I can survive. I like the unexpected, the unpredictable."

When he looked across at her this time, there was a faint challenge in his expression. "Just the way you do, princess."

She regarded him incredulously. "Me? This is not my idea of a dream vacation, much less a life-style. I told you I want white picket fences and rosebushes in the yard. I'd be perfectly content if my biggest challenge for the rest of my days was crabgrass."

He chuckled. "I don't think so. You got too much satisfaction out of reminding me that you could have managed that escape entirely on your own. You'd be bored to tears in suburbia fighting your way to the bed-linen department at a January white sale."

Suddenly Cara was tired. She could see where the conversation was headed, and she knew it didn't bode well for their future. "Maybe so. Maybe I have idealized suburbia. But there's a vast difference between knowing I can handle anything and wanting to test my

limits constantly the way you do, the way Scottie used
to do. I don't want a life with Crocodile Dundee. I
just want something that's..." She threw up her
hands in frustration. "I don't know. Normal, maybe.
What would be so bad about living a quiet, normal
life with 2.3 kids or whatever it is and a husband who
comes home on time without somebody hot on his
trail with a shotgun?"

"Nothing. That life is fine for a lot of people,
princess." There was a sad note in his voice that
chilled her.

"Well, then?"

"Not for me."

Tears stung her eyes and she refused to look at him.
He'd only said what she'd known from the first instant she'd seen him, when he'd been standing by the
Usumacinta River half naked, looking sexy as hell,
with a gun in his hand. She had recognized a bold,
unrepentant maverick. How the hell had she ever allowed herself to hope that she could tame him? Why,
for that matter, would she even want to?

His declaration made, Rod tried very hard to concentrate on flying. He knew they were in a very sticky
situation, and he admired the way Cara had held on
through it all. The lady had more guts than even she
realized. She was a woman who was more than equal
to living the sort of life-style he'd chosen for himself.

But the point, of course, was that she had every
intention of going back to New York and living in a
glass-and-steel jungle until the day came when some

man in a three-piece suit swept her off to Long Island. Rod hated cities, despised suits and especially detested the wide sweeps of lawn that required cutting at frequent intervals. Hell, on Long Island the damn lawns required manicuring. He ought to know. He'd cut one often enough during his marriage.

He glanced over at Cara. She was reading the flight manual and trying to work the radio. Her brow was knit in concentration, her lips pursed. As his gaze lingered on those lips, an entirely too familiar ache settled in his loins. He ignored it, but it was more difficult to ignore the constriction in the region of his heart. How in God's name was he ever going to let her go, so she could have the life she claimed to want?

"Any luck?" he inquired in an even tone that belied his churning emotions.

"I'm still hunting for the formula."

He grinned, his mood unexpectedly brightened by the mixture of irritation and determination he heard in her voice. He didn't have to let her go yet. There was today. Maybe tomorrow. The future? Well, he was a man who only believed in todays.

"The formula?" he teased.

She glared at him. "You know what I mean. The code. Signal. Whatever."

"Right. Have you considered just screaming for help?"

"It wouldn't be professional."

"Princess, we have a slight emergency here. I think they'll excuse us if we skip some of the protocol."

With a reluctant scowl, she lifted the microphone and began calling for the tower. She ran through the frequencies until they finally heard some static at least.

"Yes, come in," an accented voice eventually responded.

"We need some help in reaching the field at Tuxtla Gutierrez," she explained. She shot an apologetic look at Rod, then added, "We have an inexperienced pilot and we may need some help in landing."

"I do not understand. What has happened to your pilot? He is ill? You are flying the plane yourself?"

"No, no, the pilot is flying it. More or less," she added under her breath. Rod glowered at her disrespectful description. She grinned at him.

"It's just that he's . . ." Thankfully for his ego, she gave up trying to find a logical explanation. "It's a long story. Can you help us?"

"Of course, miss. First, you must stay very calm." He sounded as though he were speaking to a slightly demented child. Rod figured Cara would tolerate that tone for about five minutes. Maybe less.

"I am calm." She was practically shouting. Rod grinned at her. She rolled her eyes and lowered her voice. "I am very calm."

"That is good," the voice said with more of that deliberate patience. "We are able to see you on our radar. We will talk you in. There will be no need for you to reply. You must concentrate on the instructions."

Cara heaved a relieved sigh. "Thank you." She replaced the microphone.

"Tell him we need to get on a flight to Mexico City
as soon as we land."

"Rod," she protested. "I have the distinct impression we're already testing their tolerance."

"Do you want to wait around that airport until
Luis and his cohorts catch up with us?"

She picked up the microphone again. "Excuse
me."

"You are doing well, miss. There is no need for
alarm."

"I'm not alarmed. I have a rather unorthodox request."

"I do not understand."

"We must reach Mexico City as soon as possible.
It is an emergency. Could you make sure we are on the
next flight?"

"I'm sorry. That is not possible. It is due to leave
momentarily. There are schedules to be met. Besides,
there will be an inquiry when you land. There are
procedures that must be followed."

"And a ton of forms to fill out," Cara muttered.

"Please, señor." She turned on her most seductive
charm. Rod could almost visualize the collapse of the
man's defenses. He was probably hiding the book of
regulations at this very moment.

Cara's voice turned low and sultry. "It is very unusual, I know, but I would be very grateful for your
help." She glanced at Rod and he nodded at the un-

spoken question. "We will make it worth your while."

The offer was met by a lengthy silence. "I will do what I can, señorita."

From that moment on, the controller's manner became even more helpful. He gave clear, concise instructions to Rod until they could see the airport below them.

"I have cleared all other traffic for the moment," he said as he guided them into a landing pattern. He went through a checklist of the instrument panel. Rod heard the reassuring click of the landing gear being locked into place.

"You are ready?" the controller asked finally.

Cara looked at Rod. He nodded.

"We're ready."

Under the controller's guidance and Rod's instinctive handling, the plane came down as effortlessly as a hang glider. There was a jolt when the landing gear touched down and the nose dipped dangerously, but they came to a stop no more than a hundred yards from the terminal. A Mexicana jetliner was sitting at the gate. With any luck, Rod thought, that plane was bound for Mexico City.

Two grim-faced officials came across the runway to meet them.

Rod shot Cara an encouraging look. "Okay, princess, it's time to do some fast talking."

"I'll do it."

"No, you'd better leave it to me."

"Rod, I know their type."

She had a point. "If you're sure." He handed her some money. "Here. You'll need this."

She nodded. "Let's go."

When he glanced at her, he was astonished at the transformation. Though she was streaked with mud, though her hair was tangled, though her clothes were anything but the polished corporate look touted in upscale fashion magazines, she was suddenly the haughty businesswoman who'd turned up at his camp less than two weeks ago. She emerged from the plane with a smile on her face, her hand outstretched.

"Gentlemen," she said smoothly, allowing just a hint of smoldering sensuality into her voice. It was a combination that could have wilted stronger, more powerful men than these midlevel bureaucrats. "We can't tell you how grateful we are. Your controller has saved our lives. We would like to see that he is generously rewarded."

There was a tiny crack in the icy reception. "This has been most unusual, señorita. You would care to explain what has happened?"

"Actually, we would love to, but as we told your excellent air-traffic controller, we have an emergency. We must get to Mexico City at once."

"We have held the plane, señorita. It can wait long enough for explanations."

Rod watched as she deftly passed the folded bill to each of them. She carried off the bribery as coolly as if it were something she did every day.

Two sets of avaricious eyes widened at the denomination of the currency. The men exchanged a glance. "It is against all regulations."

"I realize that. That is why I am so grateful." She held two additional bills tantalizingly out of reach.

"I suppose it would be possible for you to speak to the authorities in Mexico City."

"Thank you. That would be perfect." The smile never faltered for an instant as she handed over the additional cash.

Their escort whizzed them into the terminal, to the gate and onto the plane in record time. With the officials to smooth their way, Rod didn't even have to explain why he was carrying a loaded gun in his flight bag.

It was only when they were in their seats and the plane was in the air that Cara turned to him and said, "That was disgusting."

"Just business, princess. You're a natural."

"I hope you don't expect me to take that as a compliment."

He grinned. "Whatever. Now, let's talk about our friend Pedro."

"Yes, let's do discuss that slime Luis. Until we got sidetracked by your stunt flying, I meant to inquire just how that man got onto the WHS payroll."

"He's a charter pilot. We keep him on retainer for Mexico and Central America."

"Apparently someone else does, too."

"Any idea who it might be?"

"None, but at least I understand how he fits in. He must be the one who gets the relics across the border."

The stewardess approached with a drink cart. Rod got them each a Scotch and waited for her to move on before asking, "You still don't think he's behind the smuggling, though, do you?"

"No. I heard him talking with Tomas about the *jefe*. He hates him as much as Tomas does. He's just a little more cowardly about openly defying him."

"Which leaves us right back where we started."

"Does it really matter? Can't we just tell the authorities what we know, hop on the next plane for the States and forget all of this?"

"I like resolutions." He lowered his voice and asked, "Besides, can you really forget those Mayan ruins so easily?"

He was asking much more, and they both knew it. He was pleading with her to remember in every sensual detail their time together. Cara refused to meet his eyes.

They made the rest of the flight in silence. Not even the second Scotch was enough to numb his nerves to the astonishing effect of her rejection. She was going to fly out of Mexico and put the whole experience behind her, him included. It hurt. It hurt like hell and, worse, he didn't know why. He should be grateful. He should be thanking his lucky stars that he'd escaped love one more time unscathed.

The problem was, of course, he hadn't.

* * *

In Mexico City, Rod bought vouchers for the cab ride to the Museum of Anthropology as Cara stood by. He certainly wasn't wasting any time. Now that he knew where things stood between them, he probably couldn't wait to see her leave so he could get on to the next adventure.

On the plane she'd chewed her lower lip so hard that she was surprised it hadn't bled. At least she hadn't cried. Now she was clenching her teeth so hard that her jaw ached.

Just let me get back to New York before I make a fool of myself, she prayed as the cab drew to a stop on Paseo de la Reforma at the side of the museum.

"This is it, princess. You all set?"

"It would have been nice to have a shower first," she grumbled with a sudden attack of feminine conceit. A dress, a silky camisole next to her skin, a dash of perfume—the mere thought was heavenly.

"Until we've actually exposed this little smuggling operation, we are still in danger. But I promise the minute we take care of this, we'll find a nice hotel and stand under the shower for hours."

The statement was disgustingly devoid of any sexual innuendo. Apparently he planned separate but equal showers.

In the vast museum lobby, the guard took one look at their bedraggled appearance and suggested they leave at once. Rod took him to one side, and whatever he said had an instantaneous effect. Cara noticed that no money changed hands, either.

Leaving them where they were, the guard went to a phone and made a call. When he returned, he told them that someone in the National Institute of Anthropology and History would see them at once, and gave them directions to the office.

Whey they found the room, Rod knocked briskly.

"Come in."

They opened the door and discovered Jorge Melendez seated behind the desk, a twisted smile on his aristocratic face.

"So," he said. "You are here at last. I have been expecting you."

Chapter Thirteen

For one brief, foolish moment Cara was grateful to find a familiar, trusted face in that room. Despite the oddly desperate expression on his face, she actually believed Jorge meant to help them. Only when Rod tensed beside her, his shoulders going rigid, his expression hardening, did she begin to realize her own naïveté.

"Come on, Cara," he said, clasping a firm hand around her wrist. "I think there's been some mistake."

"No, Señor Craig," Jorge said coldly, his voice unbelievably menacing. There was no pretense of charm.

The truth registered with Cara at last. Jorge had been behind everything, the sabotage, Diablo's death, her own kidnapping. In that instant, for the first time in her life, she knew the awful disappointment that went with betrayal, the hot fire of hatred, the urgent desire for revenge.

Jorge moved to the door and closed it behind them, cutting off the one route of escape from the suddenly too-small office. The lock turned with a quiet, well-oiled click. Cara felt her stomach muscles tighten, her hands clench. She forced herself to ignore the anger that raged through her, to put on a facade of friendly composure. Holding herself erect and still, she waited.

"There has been no mistake," he said. "You feel you have important information, according to the guard. I am here to take that information."

Though she would have preferred to remain standing, Rod practically pushed Cara into a chair, then settled down into the one next to her. His relaxed, insolent posture gave the appearance of a man totally in control of the situation, a man more than willing to be reasonable.

With one surreptitious glance Cara dispelled that carefully calculated illusion. She recognized the cold, dangerous fury in his eyes.

"But you already know everything I have to say, don't you?" he said to Jorge.

"Perhaps. Why don't you begin and we will see where our knowledge differs?"

"If you have no objections, Jorge, why don't we call one of the institute's investigators in, or perhaps someone from the legal department? I'd like to hear what they have to say about that site we stumbled across in the jungle.''

Jorge's dark eyes narrowed. ''If that is your idea of a joke, señor, then it is a bad one. Perhaps you do not realize that it is I who am in control, not those fools Tomas or Luis, who could be tricked by a mere woman.''

Cara did not waste time being insulted by the scathing description. She stared at the young archaeologist as if he were a stranger. How had she ever thought he was charming? There was a cunning about him now that she should have recognized from years of watching unscrupulous business competitors.

''And I am no woman,'' Rod reminded him.

Jorge smiled, the effect somehow chilling. ''No. You are most definitely a man and I think a very wise and pragmatic one. I think, once you have had time to consider, you will see the need for cooperation. It will only benefit all of us.''

His pointed gaze at Cara sent a shiver through her. Rod did not react visibly to the implied threat, but again she could see the glint of ice in his eyes. Jorge was pushing him close to the edge.

''Do Rafael and Maria know of your duplicity?'' Rod asked.

Jorge laughed at that. ''So that worries you, does it? Do you really think they would have allowed me to stay had they known? Your doubts would insult them. No, *amigo*, you will be relieved to know that your friends are too pure for that. Besides, it served my purpose well to keep them in the dark. After all, their idealistic protests worked to my advantage. And being in their camp, so to speak, enabled me to know at all times where the expedition was, to assure myself that they would not stumble onto my own very lucrative find.''

Ironically, Cara felt only relief at his admission. He had cleared Rafael and Maria. They were guilty of nothing more than speaking out on behalf of their own ideals and, perhaps, an unhappy willingness to accept the benefits of some unknown terrorist's violence.

"How, Jorge?" Cara asked at last. "How did you get Rafael to hire you?"

"I have the credentials he sought in an assistant. I have the knowledge, the degrees, the credibility. I worked very hard to see to that. I have worked here in the Museum. I have written papers on my research. There was no reason for Rafael and Maria to suspect that I was anything other than a hardworking archaeologist, a dedicated colleague."

Somehow she found that even more appalling than discovering he was just a simple thief. "But as an archaeologist, how can you bear to see such treasure leave the country? That discovery would have brought you international renown."

His expression hardened and he leaned toward her. "And would renown have put food into the bellies of my children? Would it have gotten medical treatment for the people of my village? Would my success have given my father back the pride that was taken from him by the government, when it nationalized his bank and robbed him of his land? The money does that, señorita, and does it very well.''

The bitterness over what had happened to his family, combined with an inherent greed had obviously stripped Jorge of all reason. That, Cara realized, made him doubly dangerous. Everything up until now had been child's play compared to this moment of confrontation. He could not allow them to leave this room, though rationally he could not conceivably hope to hide their deaths if they took place here in such a public facility. If they could convince him of that, if they could get him to take them out of here, they might have a chance.

Rod's mind was apparently working along the same lines because he suggested a deal.

''Why don't you let Cara go? This time you'll have me as your hostage. WHS is her company. She can stop the dam.''

Cara prepared to fight the idea of leaving Rod behind, but then the sense of it sank in. Jorge would never allow them both to leave. But if one of them were freed, at least they would be in a position to get help.

''And why would she want to do that, señor?''

''Because I believe it should be stopped,'' she answered for herself, not feigning the response simply for his benefit. She believed the decision was the right one. ''The cost is too high. The effect on the rain forest, the loss of Mayan history, the toll is simply too great. I could not recommend that the government proceed.''

"And if they disagree with your idealistic motives, will you build it anyway? There is, I understand, much money involved."

"The money is unimportant. WHS will not accept the contract. They will have to hire another company, conduct another survey. The dam will be delayed for months, perhaps years. Your work..." She almost choked on the word. "Your project will be safe."

Cara held her breath, praying that Jorge would take the bait. He smiled at her.

"And what is to prevent you from revealing my discovery the moment you leave this room?"

"You will have me," Rod reminded him.

"And that is enough to guarantee her silence?" Jorge scoffed. "I think, perhaps, you flatter yourself."

"No," Cara said and looked directly into Rod's eyes, then back to Jorge.

"I love him," she said quietly to the archaeologist. "So, you see, you will hold the ultimate weapon against me."

Rod listened to the words roll off Cara's tongue so easily. They were like a blow below the belt, all the more painful because he knew they were a mockery. Still, he gave her a subtle nod of encouragement. She was playing the scene exactly right. He wanted her out of here, no matter the cost to himself. One on one, he could deal with Jorge. With Cara in the room, his hands were tied. He would do nothing to put her at risk.

Jorge seemed tempted by the arrangement. With Rod's nerves stretched taut and Cara sitting on the edge of her seat, the archaeologist paced the room. Finally, he stopped behind Cara's chair, his hands dropping onto her shoulders as if daring Rod to react. All of the color drained from her face. It took every ounce of control Rod possessed to keep from going for the man's throat. Only the sight of those hands so close to Cara's neck kept him in check.

"Let her go, Jorge," he said evenly. "She will do whatever you ask."

"I do not like leaving my fate in the hands of a woman."

"You have little choice, unless you're prepared to kill us both here and now."

Jorge hesitated still. Then, at last, he nodded decisively and Rod's muscles began to relax. "I will do it." His fingers stroked meaningfully along the column of Cara's neck, raising goose bumps on the satiny skin. "But I will be watching you, Señorita Scott. One mistake and I will kill the man you claim to love."

Rod caught the hastily masked look of panic in her eyes. "There will be no mistakes," she assured Jorge. "I will arrange a meeting with the officials this afternoon and give them a verbal report recommending against the dam."

"And then you will leave the country at once."

With a quick, anxious glance at Rod, she nodded. "On the first available flight."

At least she would be safe then, Rod thought. His own fate was of less consequence. Satisfied with the negotiations, the tension finally began to drain out of him, but not that alertness that kept him from trusting Jorge entirely.

With Jorge's blessing, Cara rose and went to the door. He turned the key in the lock for her, then took her arm in a grip that was bound to leave bruises on the pale skin. Rod grasped the arms of his chair so tightly he could feel the metal digging into his flesh.

"No mistakes," Jorge warned one last time.

Cara swallowed hard, but her expression remained cool, professional. Though Rod tried to send her one final signal, she avoided his gaze. "You need not worry."

Then she was gone and, though the door was once more locked, the odds, once again, had turned in his favor. He took advantage of Jorge's momentary distraction to reach for his flight bag. A kick sent it skittering across the floor beyond his reach.

"Do not be a fool. Even your woman would not be so stupid as to cross me."

Then Jorge made his first mistake. He deliberately goaded him. "She is not unattractive. It is too bad she feels as she does about you or I might have had her for my own mistress."

A surge of pure rage tore through Rod and sent him to his feet. He reached Jorge before the man had time to react, his fist connecting with that arrogant face with a satisfying crunch. He had just leveled another powerful blow at the man's stomach when he felt the press of cold metal against his own gut. It brought him up short. He knew better than to argue with a weapon at close range.

"Kill me and you lose your hold over Cara," he said quite calmly. The muscles across his shoulders were bunched into knots, but his heart drummed with a surprisingly steady beat. He held his breath, though, and eventually Jorge backed down, eyes blazing furiously.

"Do not tempt me again, señor. I can always find the woman and see that she maintains her silence."

Rod dropped back into a chair and managed a neutral expression. "So, what happens now? We can't stay locked in this room forever. Sooner or later, they'll want to empty the trash cans or dust the desk or something."

"We will leave, when I say so," Jorge said edgily.

"And go where?"

Rod pushed because he could see that Jorge had not thought this through beyond the moment. Rod wanted Jorge off balance, wanted his nerves on the verge of cracking under the stress. Already there were white lines of tension at the corners of his mouth. Fear glazed his eyes. Rod took his measure of the man and knew it was only hours until he broke. He had no intention of waiting that long to make his own escape.

"You will see when the time comes," Jorge snapped.

Rod shrugged with indifference. "I don't suppose you could get us some coffee in here in the meantime. It's been a hell of a morning."

Jorge regarded him as if he'd just suggested they import drugs.

Rod persisted persuasively. "What could possibly be wrong with asking a secretary to bring in a couple of cups of coffee? Everyone knows you're in the middle of an important meeting. It would be natural to want coffee, perhaps even some sandwiches. You look like you could use the meal as well as I could."

He watched as Jorge struggled with himself. Eventually he must have decided that Rod's request would buy him some much-needed time. He called and requested that someone bring coffee and sandwiches.

They sat waiting in silence, the strain obviously mounting. When the rap came on the door, Jorge jumped, then rose and went to open it.

But instead of a secretary with lunch, he found Rafael and Maria.

And, then, all hell broke loose.

Rod took advantage of their unexpected arrival to leap from his chair. Hearing the movement, Jorge grabbed for his gun, only to have it wrenched from his grasp by Rafael as Maria screamed. Rod whirled the young archaeologist around and delivered another blow to his face, then one to his chin and another that split the skin above his eye. He was just getting started.

It took Rafael and two guards to pull Rod off of Jorge.

"You have won, my friend," Rafael said, gently guiding him back to a chair. Rod's pulse was pounding, his knuckles scraped and bleeding, his need for revenge unsatisfied. It was Cara's voice that drew him back from his blind outrage.

"I was rather hoping you'd wait for me before pummelling the man," she said.

Drawing in a deep breath, he looked up into amused blue eyes. "Take your best shot, princess. I doubt the guards would object."

She shook her head. "It seems anticlimactic somehow."

Instead, she moved to his side and knelt down, resting her head on his thigh. A sigh shuddered through her. "Are you okay?"

He stroked her hair. "Never better."

"Promise?"

"You know me. I never lie...even when it hurts."

Neither of them were aware when the guards took Jorge from the room.

"Leaving you here with him was the hardest thing I've ever had to do, even though I knew it was the only way I could help," Cara said.

"Thanks for sending in the reinforcements." He gave Maria and Rafael a rueful smile, as he ran a finger along Cara's cheek. He shook his head. "I should have known you wouldn't just do what you'd promised and leave town."

Maria laughed. "You must be very foolish, if you thought for one moment that she would abandon you."

He glanced away from Cara long enough to see that Maria was standing close by Rafael's side. His arm was tight around her waist. "What brought you two back?"

"I would like to say it was some great insight, but it was little more than luck," Rafael admitted. "Thanks to that talk you had with me, I finally decided it was time to put an end to the charade we have maintained for the past several years and get married. We came back to arrange for a small ceremony. We would like it very much if you two would come. Perhaps it would give you ideas as well."

Rod purposely ignored the pointed suggestion and concentrated on offering enthusiastic congratulations.

"I'm just grateful they showed up when they did," Cara said with heartfelt sincerity. "I was running through the museum like a crazy lady looking for help, when I ran into them. Fortunately, they believed me when I told them about Jorge. They had begun to wonder about his frequent absences from their site. They notified the guards. I was worried about getting past the secretary again, but she wasn't at her desk."

Rod permitted himself a slight smile. "Inadvertently, I guess I played my part as well. I had Jorge send her for sandwiches."

Suddenly Cara shuddered again. He could feel her scalding tears soaking through the cotton of his slacks. "Princess, don't, please. I hate it when you cry."

She looked up at him them, her eyes shimmering, lips trembling. Her chin lifted proudly. "Then I guess you ain't seen nothing yet. Just wait until tomorrow when you have to put me on that plane back to New York."

Rod's heart sank. So, then, she was still going and without him.

"We have tonight, though," he said with feigned enthusiasm. "Let's make it a good one."

Hand in hand, they left the museum with Rafael and Maria. After promising to attend the wedding, they were dropped off at a small, quiet hotel that promised enough hot water to wipe away days of grime, if not the memories. They shared the shower, after all. And then the bed. And then a delicious candlelight dinner. For Cara, there was a bittersweet agony to all of it.

How could two people so much in love hurt each other so? And she didn't doubt that Rod loved her. She'd seen the emotion shining in his eyes, felt it in the tenderness of his touch, the joy of their union.

Now as they lay together, her head resting on his chest, his arms tight around her, she knew the true meaning of serenity and contentment. She also knew it would die, if they forced their love to fit the mold either of them had chosen for their lives.

She tangled her fingers in the curls of hair on his chest, then pressed a kiss to the spot above his heartbeat, aware of the precise moment when it accelerated.

"Up here, princess," he said in a ragged whisper.

She moved to meet his lips with her own, then tasted the salt of tears. His? Her own? It didn't really matter. They both knew what they were doing was right. It made sense. It was the only way.

And no matter how often they said it or thought it, it still hurt like hell.

The only thing that didn't hurt was this rush of feeling when their lips met, when his hand moved along the sweep of her back, the curve of her hips. The strokes and caresses—deep, powerful, intense— muted pain and brought an exquisite joy in its place.

The first time they'd made love, deep in the jungle, had been filled with the passionate hunger of newly discovered desire. Earlier tonight, there had been the urgency of two people who had survived and needed to prove that life went on. Now...now was the slow building of a tempest, a gentle reaffirmation destined to explode with the same heat of those other times. There was nothing tame about the two of them, nothing tame about their love.

Cara relished the wildness, even as she knew it had no place in her life. She would remember it, cherish it, but she would let it go. Tomorrow.

In the meantime, she soared with it.

Everything about the morning was painful. The sun shone too brightly for a day of goodbyes. Cara thought if Rod touched her just once she would shatter into a million pieces. They had said everything there was to say, except the words that would have kept them together.

When the phone rang, they both jumped. Rod reached it first.

"Yes, hello."

Cara watched his face as he listened, saw the quick glance he cast in her direction. His jaw tensed. His complexion turned pale. Her pulse began to beat unsteadily.

"I understand," Rod was saying. "Are you okay? Yes, she's here, but I'll tell her. We'll be on the next flight."

Cara grabbed for the phone then, but Rod decisively held it out of reach and pushed the button to disconnect the call.

"What the hell is wrong with you?" she demanded, infuriated by his peremptory manner. Then she saw the bleak expression in his eyes and her heart stood still. "What is it?"

"It's Scottie," he said very, very quietly.

Cara felt a flood of tears in her eyes. She choked back a sob and looked at him. "Is he . . . ?"

"No." His hands were on her shoulders, reassuring, comforting. Still she shook.

"He is not dead," he insisted. "But he has had another heart attack. He's back in intensive care. Louise thinks you'd better come right away."

Cara nodded and blindly moved to pick up her already packed bags.

"Cara?"

"What?"

"Are you all right?"

"I'll manage."

She felt his fingers on her chin, felt him lift her face up until she had no choice but to look into his sympathetic eyes. "You don't have to handle this alone, princess."

"Yes, I do. I always have."

An unreadable expression crossed his face. "Not this time," he said decisively. "I'm coming with you."

Chapter Fourteen

Cara clung to Rod's hand all the way to New York. Though she'd offered up a token argument when he'd announced his decision to come with her and though she seemed oblivious to him otherwise, there was her hand securely wrapped around his. Rod realized during that endless flight, if he hadn't known it before, that his impulsive decision had been the right one. As painful as it might be to say goodbye all over again when the crisis with Scottie was past, he would not have been able to live with himself if he'd left her to face it alone.

Besides, he loved Scottie, too. Like a wayward son who hadn't been home nearly enough, he was filled with regrets for time wasted. Rod knew he should have been to see Scottie before this. If the old man died before Rod had had a chance to tell him how much he cared, he'd have to live with that forever. At that thought, Rod's throat closed up and his eyes misted with unshed tears.

At Kennedy Airport, he saw that they made it through customs in record time. He guided Cara to the limousine that Louise had waiting. And then, despite her furious glare, he instructed the driver to swing by Cara's apartment.

"You look like hell, princess."

"Thank you very much, but I'm not going to a charity ball."

"Maybe not, but you need makeup and one of your brightest dresses. You'll feel better, and it'll cheer Scottie up to see you looking good. You don't want him to realize what an ordeal you've been through, do you?"

She shot him a nasty look. "You're just worried he'll blame it on you."

"Could be," he said.

She dropped the argument.

When she emerged from her bedroom a half hour later, he could see at once that the break had been just what she needed. A soft blush colored her pale cheeks, makeup hid the worried lines around her eyes, and a cool cotton sundress in a bold shade of turquoise made her look spectacular, even if she didn't feel it.

"Better," he commented, his heart turning over at the shadows in her eyes that no amount of sprucing up could banish. He held out his hand. "Now let's go see to it that your father gets well."

As they pulled up outside the hospital, Cara turned to him, stripped for once of her brave facade. Her lower lip quivered. "What if he doesn't?"

The doubts, the forlorn look in her eyes, tore at him. He squeezed her hand. "He will, princess. He has everything to live for."

But when they reached the intensive care unit, not even Rod's optimism could counter the ominous hum of activity. Louise was waiting for them just outside, her dark hair uncharacteristically mussed, her flawless makeup long since gone. Cara hesitated, then squared her shoulders and moved forward with a brisk, confident step. Rod had never been prouder of her.

"How is he?" she asked as the older woman embraced her.

"They say it'll be at least another twenty-four hours before we'll know for sure. If..." Louise's voice shook. She took a deep breath and drew herself up. Rod noticed that there was compassion and reassurance in her eyes as they met Cara's. The two women were united in their love for Scottie.

"If he makes it that long, he has a chance. The doctors aren't trying to gloss this over. Obviously, it doesn't help that he just went through another attack a few weeks ago."

"It's all my fault," Cara whispered, her shoulders slumping. The fight seemed to drain right out of her.

Louise and Rod exchanged a look. "How on earth do you figure that, princess?"

"If I hadn't gone away..."

"He would just have worried about something else. Now stop it."

She turned an angry gaze on him. "Why should I listen to you? You're the one I had to go chasing after."

The accusation stung, just as she'd known it would. Rod paled, his jaw tightening. This time it was Louise who stepped in.

"Stop it, Cara," she said firmly. "If anyone's to blame, it's Scottie himself. He wouldn't listen. Do you know I actually caught him with a cigar about ten minutes after you got on that plane to Mexico? I'm surprised the whole room didn't go up in flames with all the oxygen they had in there."

That brought a faint smile to Cara's lips. He noticed she had already chewed off most of her lipstick. "When can I see him?"

"Same rules as before. One visitor at a time. Ten minutes every hour. It's almost time. You go in. I'm sure he's tired of seeing my face by now. He'll be glad to know you're home."

Rod reached out and clasped Louise's hand as Cara approached the intensive care unit door, glancing impatiently at her watch.

"You're a hell of a woman," he said gently.

"I love them both."

"I think they know that."

They sat there, watching helplessly as Cara paced.

"She's ready to crack," he said softly to Louise.

The secretary surveyed him knowingly, then smiled. "She's stronger than you think. She'll be better once she's seen him. How are you holding up?"

"Me? Don't you remember? I'm the coldhearted man who lets disasters roll off his back, the womanizer who never sticks around long enough to see the damage he's caused."

"I, for one, never believed that nonsense," Louise retorted.

"Then you're in a minority."

"Does Cara believe it?"

"Actually, no. That's not the problem."

"Then what is? One look in your eyes and I can see you love her. I'd have to guess she feels the same way or I'd never have found her in your hotel room in Mexico. She doesn't take such things lightly."

"You always were a shrewd woman, Louise. There's just one hitch. Cara and I don't want the same things."

"If you start out wanting each other badly enough, time has a way of taking care of the rest." She smiled at him. "Scottie will be pleased. He guessed, you know. He told me after he talked to you both in Mexico that you two were in love. Scared the daylights out of him that you both might be too stubborn to admit it."

Rod grinned. "You don't suppose he staged this heart attack just to get us here, where he could have a hand in manipulating things to suit himself?"

She laughed at that. "I wouldn't put it past him."

"Then I know he's going to live. He won't want to miss seeing how it all turns out."

It was worse this time than before. Knowing what to expect when she walked through the doorway to see Scottie still hadn't prepared Cara for the sight of all those tubes and monitors being back again. She knew what every piece of equipment implied, and none of it was good.

He looked even more diminished now than he had when she'd left for Mexico. In less than two weeks he'd lost more weight, his cheeks were sunken, his complexion bloodless. There was none of the spirit and fight she remembered from childhood, none of the determination she'd seen after the last attack.

She blinked back tears and swallowed terror. "Scottie," she whispered. "I'm back."

Blue eyes blinked open, registered her presence and closed again on a sigh. She took his huge, callused hand in her own and held it to her cheek.

"Get well, damn you. I need you. Rod's going to take off and leave me. If you die, I won't have anybody."

A tear rolled down her cheek. "He's so like you, Scottie," she whispered. "It would be like losing you twice, and I couldn't take that. We both know how stubborn you can be, so that means you can beat this. You've got me waiting for you, and Louise and a company. I don't want to run WHS one minute longer than I have to. I nearly made a mess of it in Mexico, but Rod and I did okay in the end. Actually, we make a pretty good team, but I suspect you knew we would.''

A nurse touched her shoulder. ''I'm sorry, miss, but you'll have to leave now.''

''But I just got back. There's so much I need to tell him.''

''He needs his rest now. You'll be able to tell him later.''

Later. She clung to the word as some sort of talisman. There would be a later.

The days that followed passed in a haze of uncertainty. Cara moved between the hospital and her apartment with no real awareness of when the transitions took place, only that Rod executed them with quiet insistence. He dropped her off at the hospital each morning at eight, after insisting that she eat breakfast and standing over her until she'd finished it. He returned at six and sat with her through the evening, before taking her and Louise out for dinner. She had no idea where he went in between.

They had been back in New York a week before she realized how thoroughly enmeshed he had become in her life. He moved around her apartment as though he belonged there, and she found that she liked the intimacy of finding his razor by the bathroom sink, his shirts hanging in the closet. Most of all she liked waking in his arms, feeling his strength surround her and give her the courage to get through another day. It was a make-believe world, but she didn't have the will to fight it.

Scottie was improving bit by tiny bit. The doctors were cautiously optimistic. She clung to every shred of hope they offered. It got her through the days. Rod got her through the nights.

Now it was barely 6:00 a.m. and he was still sprawled across the bed, arms outflung, one leg draped across hers. She grinned and wondered how he had ever managed on a cot, much less in a hammock. He was one of those people who would have made even a king-size bed seem too small. She thought about the contrast between his very masculine presence and her very feminine decor. He'd taken one look at the frills their first night here and his lips had twitched with amusement. Until that moment, she'd never noticed how many ruffles and tucks and flowers there were from bedspread to drapes to lamp shades. Perhaps it was time to redecorate, she thought, then brought herself up short. Why? Rod would be gone soon.

She sighed and his arms came around her.

"You're awake early," he mumbled sleepily. "What are you thinking about?"

She curved happily into the embrace. "Ruffles."

His eyes snapped open at that. "I beg your pardon."

"I was just thinking how cute you look surrounded by all these ruffles."

"Cute?" His lips found the precise spot on her neck that set her wild.

She groaned. "I take it back. You are wonderful. Handsome. Sexy."

"But not cute."

Her back arched as his mouth sought out her breast. "Definitely…oh…not…oh, Rod…cute."

He grinned at her and sprang out of bed. "Thank you. Now let's hustle. I want to spend a few minutes with Scottie this morning, too, before I get started on my day."

Cara sat up and drew her knees to her chest and watched him move around the room, his lithe body as graceful and exciting as a tiger's. "That reminds me. I've been meaning to ask you where you're spending your days."

"At the office," he said and shut himself in the bathroom.

Cara stared after him, openmouthed. She was still sitting like that when he emerged from his shower wearing nothing more than a towel and a smile.

"Explain."

He stared at her blankly, removed the towel from around his waist and used it to dry his hair. Admittedly, it was one hell of a distraction, but Cara wasn't allowing him off the hook that easily.

"You said you've been going to the office."

"Where else would I go?"

She shrugged. "I don't know. I hadn't really thought about it. What do you do there?"

He laughed. "Princess, if you don't know what an engineer does at WHS, then no one does."

She shook her head. "I know I sound dense, but I never thought of you actually sitting down in an office behind a desk."

"I don't do it all that often, but that doesn't mean I can't when the need arises, and it seemed to me that the need had arisen. Louise said there were decisions that had to be made, and neither of us wanted to bother you with them. She helped out the first couple of days just to be sure I knew the routine."

That really silenced her. "Wait a minute," she said finally. "You're actually running WHS?"

"Someone has to," he said nonchalantly. "Scottie certainly can't and with everything else you have to handle right now, you're not up to it. Don't worry, princess, I'm just keeping your chair warm. You can have it back the minute you're ready."

"I don't give a damn about getting my chair back. I'm just astounded. I thought you hated this sort of thing."

Rod looked uncomfortable. "This is an emergency."

She studied him closely. He didn't look all that miserable. "How do you feel about the work, though?" she asked cautiously.

"It's work," he replied evasively. "Now come on and get moving. There's a lot of it to do and I want to get started."

She actually thought she heard a note of excitement in his voice and her heart flipped over.

Over the next weeks the pattern varied hardly at all, except that Scottie began an astonishing recovery. By the end of July he was barking orders at everyone again and demanding to be released from the hospital.

"Only if you come home with me," Cara insisted, then caught the look that passed between her father and Louise. "Never mind."

"I'll take good care of him," Louise promised.

"I know that."

"Then why the scowl?" Scottie demanded. "Don't tell me you don't approve, because I know different."

Cara and Louise both blushed. "It's not that."

"What then?"

"I guess I was just counting on your being at my place when . . ." She couldn't finish the sentence.

Scottie completed it for her. "When Rod leaves."

She nodded miserably.

"Come here and sit beside your old man."

Cara went and perched on the edge of the bed. He took her hand in his.

"There's something I've been meaning to talk to you about."

"About Rod?"

"Yes. How would you feel about me taking on a partner?"

Her eyes lit up with excitement. Then she shook her head. "He'll never do it."

"He's already agreed to . . . if it's okay with you."

Cara was astonished. "You've discussed it with him?"

"Actually it was his idea. Seemed to think it might solve some other problems he was having. I don't suppose you know anything about those?"

"Yes." She felt like shouting. She threw her arms around Scottie. "I love you."

"I know that, but I'm not the one you ought to be saying those words to. I think there's a fellow over at the office who needs to hear 'em a whole lot more than I do."

She grinned at him and hugged Louise. "I'm on my way."

At the door to Scottie's office, she hesitated. Rod was sitting behind her father's desk, his sleeves rolled up to reveal muscular forearms from which his tan was fading. He was chewing on the end of a pen and staring pensively out the window at the skyscrapers beyond. He didn't look happy. Her heart sank. What if this wasn't what he wanted after all?

She went up behind his chair and put her arms around his neck. "A penny for your thoughts."

He twirled the chair around and pulled her onto his lap. "They're worth much more."

He drew her head down for a long, breath-stealing kiss. "That's what I was thinking about."

"I like the way your mind works. Any other ideas?"

"Plenty, but your father would fire me if I tried any of them out here."

"That's not the way I hear it."

Hazel eyes regarded her closely. "He told you?"

She nodded. "Is it what you really want?"

He sighed and tightened his arms around her. "Remember when you told me about wanting to follow in Scottie's footsteps? You said you'd discovered later that you were actually good at it."

"I remember."

"Well, that's what I've found out these past few weeks, too. I'm every bit as good in this office as I am out in the field."

She touched a finger to his lips. "I never doubted for a minute that you'd be good at anything you decided to do. The question is do you like it?"

"Surprisingly enough, I do. I'm not sure I could take a steady diet of it, but with the agreement Scottie and I have worked out, I wouldn't have to. I'll split my time between fieldwork and New York, depending on . . ." His words faltered.

"Depending on what?"

"Things."

"What things?"

Amusement lurked in the depths of his eyes and his lips formed a half smile. "You couldn't let me do this the conventional way, could you?"

She looked at him blankly. "Do what?"

"Propose. I actually had reservations for a fancy restaurant tonight. I'd ordered the finest champagne. I even put in a request for a full moon. I wanted all the romantic props."

"You don't need them."

This time she got a full-fledged grin. "Does that mean you want to hear my speech now? I have this one about compromise and love and commitment and white picket fences. It's in my pocket.''

She grinned back at him. ''I'd settle for one that gets to the point.''

''Will you marry me?''

''And be your partner?''

''Actually I'll be Scottie's partner.''

She hit him. ''You know what I mean.''

''Will you be my partner and friend and lover?''

''You left off wife.''

''You weren't listening, princess. As usual. That was the original question.''

''In that case, I accept.''

''Don't you want to think about it?''

''And give you time to change your mind? Not a chance.''

''It will be okay, princess, I promise you. We'll make it work.''

''I know we will.''

''Starting now.'' He stood up and carried her across the office, then kicked the door shut. He took an extra five seconds to flip the lock.

''I thought you had dinner reservations.''

''I do.'' His lips were hot and demanding as they swept along her jaw, across her brow. ''Later.''

''Shouldn't we get dressed?'' The words came out on a breathless sigh.

''Undressed is better.''

He proved his point by slipping her blouse off her shoulders. Her skirt slid to the floor. Her insides quivered as his hands moved over her.

"Undressed is definitely better," she concurred. It was the last thing she said for a very long time.

Shadows filled the office and turned to darkness. Murmured words and quiet sighs filled the air. With Rod's body pressed to hers on the narrow sofa, Cara suddenly began chuckling.

"What's so funny?"

"I was just wondering about something. Do you suppose Scottie and Louise ever..."

"Cara!" He silenced her with a kiss.

They never did get to dinner.

*   *   *   *   *